LOVE IN THE TIME OF THE IMPROVISED EXPLOSIVE DEVICE

JR POMERANTZ

INVITATION

Don't be a stranger! Let's have a visit at
www.jrpomerantz.com.

For Anandi

1

I OPENED JUNK

I opened junk drawer number one: no.

Junk drawer number two: not in here. Maybe I was wrong.

Third and final junk drawer?

There it was.

I thought Elise had been storing our hammer in a new spot, but I couldn't quite place where. Why did she have so many junk drawers, only to use them for storing things that

a. weren't junk, and

b. had a clear location elsewhere?

7:30 pm.

Elise used to give the kids a bath around this time, and I was sick of noting it, day after day. I heaved myself off the couch.

It was time to do something about it.

I ran upstairs to the bathroom. Not as fast as that other day. I slammed open the door, I raised the hammer over my head, and I brought it down on the side of the bathtub

that day the water spilled out over the top and onto the floor, the water and the—

as hard as I could. Nothing happened.

No hairline fracture. Not even a chip.

It was resilient.

I didn't need this bathtub anymore.

No Elise. No kids. Every night when 7:30 pm rolled around, I came up here. Stared into its depths like I would learn something. And you know what? I never learned anything.

The hammer was worthless. I needed something bigger.

I headed for the garage, paused in the kitchen. I rearranged the magnets that held a fingerpainting on the refrigerator.

James had loved painting but Allison hadn't quite taken to it yet. She would start out with confidence—get her cute little fingers all painted up, and just stand there. Considering her composition, I suppose. Hell, I don't know. Then she'd cry when the paint dried on her fingers without making it to the paper.

This one, though. This painting had been a breakthrough. Her first work of art without tears.

I moved on.

She'd just turned three.

I turned my back on the painting, and I moved on.

In the garage, behind Ally's tricycle, I spotted it: our sledge-hammer from the basement finishing fiasco of six years ago.

Back upstairs.

I raised it up over my head and brought it down hard on that close side, the rim where the water had spilled over that day. It was overflowing when I opened the door. That day.

An eyeball-sized chunk chipped off.

It was a start.

I kept working, kept smashing, kept bringing that sledgehammer down, my arms were on fire, but let's be honest about who I am, they would have been anyway, from the least little exertion. I kept going until the bathtub broke into three. Three pieces.

I had to keep going, keep smashing. I could hardly breathe after I finished pulverizing the first piece. Bathtub dust all around me. I thought to flick on the fan switch, but it was weak. Barely worked. One more thing I was supposed to fix and didn't.

I moved through the second piece, then the third, until they were dust. Every bit of that bathtub was destroyed, pipes coming out of the wall that led nowhere now. Dust stuck to every part of me, went in my mouth and I tasted it. The sweat rolled off, white ceramic mixed in, sliding off my face. I dropped the sledgehammer, swept that sweat off my chin.

I sat down on the floor. Rested my back up against the wall. I turned the disembodied faucet on so the water could run out onto the floor. Watched it soak the right leg of my jeans.

But no, I wouldn't sit around in there again. I'd done enough of that. I turned off the faucet, I left the sledgehammer where it lay, and I closed the door on my way out.

My wife and kids had been dead for three months. Now the bathtub where they'd died was gone, too.

Who could I blame?

Myself? The mesh? Whoever thought it was a great idea to market chicken wire to string up my wife's collapsed vagina? The company that sold the death of my whole family? The doctor who installed it? The FDA?

Yes, yes, and yes. And yes, yes, yes.

And *yes*, I still went back. Back to work at the FDA.

2

I'M SORRY, JIM

"I'm sorry, Jim."

Monday morning. I'd accidentally left my office door slightly ajar. Stephen was standing outside peering in, standard-issue hat in hand, sheepish. He'd been shipped out on Corps business for months, doing vaccinations at the border.

"What?" For an instant, I couldn't figure out what he was talking about. Isn't that wild? "Oh. Thank you." Was this the first time I'd seen him since—?

"I just heard," he said. "About—" Same expression everybody had at the funeral, gawking at one adult coffin and two child-sized coffins all lined up. Elise's elderly mom, collapsed and wailing.

"Thanks, Stephen. I really appreciate it." The fluorescent bulb in my office flickered. "I gotta call this in," I said, pointing up at the offense. "You know how long repairs take." I always had to act fast before people tied themselves up in knots trying to avoid saying anything specific. I stood up and closed the door, nodding, even bowing a little.

My family leave

family leave, get it? I'll be here all day folks

time had run out, so I was forced back into the office. Excruciating. Work was a nonstop apology tour. Everybody was sorry. As if they'd caused it. All day every day. Last week, Sharon at the front desk teared up like it was her wife and kids. Her dumb makeup ran all down her face and I was the one who felt bad. I was sick of absolving everyone of their guilt. It would be better not to see anyone at all.

On Tuesday I came to work earlier. On Wednesday I came to work even earlier than that. Seven am. Six am. Five am. I managed to get through security anonymously, without an apology, and walk the dimly lit halls to my office. I shut myself inside; I clicked on the monitor. I sat there and I waited for work.

But they had lightened my load to accommodate my grief. No requests in my inbox. Not that week.

Not that month.

Maybe the Office of Planning had been dissolved, and they had forgotten to tell me?

I settled into a routine, an invisible government employee regimen:

1. sneak into work, and
2. read the morning clips about FDA-relevant news: medical device failures, the new drugs on the market, the fake drugs on the market, an illicit organ farm chop-shopping dead bodies somewhere in the Midwest. Mass emails en masse about the network being down, this and that administrator coming or going.

After the daily clips, and the junk email du jour, I stared into space until the silence told me most of my colleagues had left for the day. Fourteen hours after entry, I cautiously emerged from my office and drove home. Sometimes a straggler intercepted me. To apologize. Again. Eventually my coworkers left me alone.

And a year passed by. As they do.

3

STUCK IN TRAFFIC

Stuck in traffic. Was it too late to slip in unnoticed?

Maybe I should have gone back home and called out. Tuesday was a busier day in the hallways, with people waking up from a Monday call-out.

No, it would be okay. Nobody would notice me. Office of Planning was so dark and silent lately, I'd been scanning the notices for months looking for evidence it even existed.

I parked our old Prius on the fringe of the massive parking lot. Newly built and already too small. You'd think an organization that regulated milk and stents could get a handle on spatial relations, wouldn't you? Maybe you don't think about it. I didn't, before.

I was so far out, I had to walk around the unexploded ordinances. The United States Food and Drug Administration used to be a weapons testing center until, one day, they accidentally detonated a ton or two of something significant. The explosion blew out the windows of all the homes in a 1.5-mile radius.

After that, the weapons testing center shipped out and we shipped in. Signs on the trails warn you not to stray.

The walk in took a while. It was usually dark when I arrived.

Everything looked different in the daylight. I wanted to say *worse*, but I couldn't tell how or why.

By the time I got through security and up to the third floor, it was my latest arrival time in years. Sharon wasn't in her usual spot at the front desk—where the hell was she? Had she moved on? Maybe there was an email about that. Her replacement glared at me the way only a spiteful federal employee can.

Wait. Was she wearing an American flag onesie?

"Happy Memorial Day," replacement Sharon said, in the least joyful voice I'd ever heard. Maybe her family died too. She quickly shifted her stare back to her phone.

"Happy Memorial Day," I said.

I'd nearly made it all the way down the hall to the safety of my office when it *happened*.

My boss.

Nicholas Chang. Deputy Director, Office of Planning, emerged from his office at exactly the moment I passed it. We locked eyes.

He looked horrified to see me, which was a great relief, because that meant I could pretend this *hadn't* happened, nod, and keep walking.

And I tried to.

"Jim!"

No.

I did my nod.

"So glad to run into you."

Oh *no*.

I kept walking.

"How are you, buddy?"

Buddy.

He tailed me until I stopped and faced him.

"Listen, got a few minutes? I need to see you in my office."

I did have a few minutes and he damn well knew it. I couldn't believe he was doing this. He took his spotless glasses off, polished them with a miniature chamois cloth he reserved for this purpose, until they were just as spotless as they had been on his face. Replaced the glasses. Replaced the chamois in his sport jacket's front pocket. He was doing the same a year ago. More productive nervous tic than an eye twitch.

Eye twitch was *my* thing.

Then he looked at me, without blinking, until I twitched and I caved.

"Sure, Nick. I'll be right over. Let me set down my things." I didn't have any things. He was kind enough not to point that out.

To date, he'd handled my situation better than anybody else—by ignoring it completely. Then ignoring *me* completely. If I hadn't been so late today, he might have ignored me for another year or three. I could only look upon this meeting—impromptu or planned—as a product of my own carelessness in allowing myself to be seen. He would never have gone the distance to knock on my door. He had more decency than that.

I was so used to being invisible, maybe a part of me had started to believe I actually couldn't be seen anymore. I guess I had gotten set in my ways.

Something Elise would have said to me. As if it's a place you get to. As if the ways had ever been *not* set at the start.

He receded down the hallway; I took a hard right. Hell, now that I'd been discovered out in the open, probably to be fired, I might as well delay it for as long as possible. Maybe I could trigger a major coronary event while I still had health insurance.

I made a break for the cafeteria to hunt down a cup of coffee, steel myself for whatever this meeting was about. They were going to RIF me right out of there. That was probably it. God knew I hadn't done anything in the past year, except read news clips. Could be they'd noticed.

I was done for. Mediocre government career completely ruined.

Goodbye, paycheck.

4

THE FDA CAMPUS

The FDA campus had changed a lot while I was hiding in my office. Half the place was under construction and the other half was brand new. They'd planted ornamental grasses on the side of Building 2. I vaguely recalled reading in one of the notices they were a haven for rats.

"I found a rat's nest in here!" Brushing little James's hair.

Elise shouted down to me from the bathroom, I must have been in the living room: our typical bedtime routine. Every time James turned around to see, Elise attempted her ridiculous rat impression.

Sometimes she would surprise tickle-attack. Well, it wasn't really a surprise. She'd say *tickle tickle tickle* while she did it. Either way, they'd both collapse in helpless laughter. And I'd listen from the couch.

It was fancy at the FDA now. Like a shittier Google. How were we funding all this? Must have been that sweet, sweet tobacco money. Start regulating cigarettes, get a dozen new buildings. Does that sound like a conflict of interest?

Nah.

I crossed the campus, nodding at the extroverts, avoiding eye contact with the introverts—that hadn't changed. The best coffee was in Building 31. Or at least, it used to be. Was I keeping Deputy Chang waiting? Probably, but he and my firing could wait.

"Jim? Jim Schneider?" A tap on the shoulder.

Ravi.

We met in new employee orientation. Ten years ago? Wow. Could that be right? Ten years. We'd seen each other quite a bit, in the old days. I'd even gone to dinner at his house, met his wife. So long ago.

"Where the hell have you been? I heard a rumor you'd joined foreign posts. Thought they'd shipped you out to China." Ravi seized me by one shoulder, grabbed my hand, pumped it up and down.

I rolled with it like it was normal, but I hadn't touched or spoken to a human in the past year. And I hadn't meant to start today.

"No, no," I said. "I've been around. Same spot, up in Planning." I pointed up, to the office that was about to oust me.

"Around, but not visible! After the long weekend, we should get coffee, catch up. Great to see you, Jim. Hey, you should stop by the lab." Ravi pointed at the double monoliths on the end of the line of indistinguishable buildings in various stages of development, beyond a brand new bronze double helix.

"Yeah, sure."

"I can show you around. Pretty fun stuff in there." Good old Ravi. Just as much energy as ten years ago. Didn't seem all that common around here, now that I thought about it. He was sharp, talked a mile a minute, that's what I'd always liked about him. Not slow and oblivious.

Lot of new artwork around here too, now that I noticed. Not the usual three-star hotel neutrals of the old days. Modern. Flashy stuff.

———

NICK'S DOOR OPENED: Leslie.

"Jim," Leslie said.

"Leslie," I said. She nodded and scurried off. Another of my colleagues who opposed eye contact. My favorite kind. Nick ushered me in, air traffic-controlled me to a chair so I could relax and enjoy my firing.

His office overlooked the new bronze double helix.

Those spirals really caught the sunlight, bounced it into the office, onto the picture of two miniature copies of Nick that sat on his desk, pointing at me.

This meeting was going to be a firing for sure. What was my strategy? I couldn't claim discrimination. Grief? Nah. You don't get to blame your dead loved ones when you don't produce at your job for a year. My palms went from clammy to clammier.

"Thanks for taking the time out," Nick said. He was flanked by a vast array of awards, certificates, degrees, and accolades. If I'd had the same, I wouldn't be getting fired.

If my wife and kids weren't dead I wouldn't be getting fired.

"Have a seat, Jim. I'll just say this directly."

I sighed deeply, but it was an act. I didn't care. Losing my job was going to be fine.

"Nick, I know what you're going to say."

"Oh, great! Who told you?"

Not being able to ever get another job was going to be fine.

"I...I could have guessed, I suppose. Based on..." I trailed off.

...me not doing anything for a year, making up my own schedule around hiding from you and everybody else in this agency, I didn't say.

Sliding into homelessness was going to be fine.

"Afghanistan's gonna be a real hub, important new post." He stood up with so much momentum that it startled me and I stood up too. I put my left eyeball right in the path of a reflected double-helix sunbeam. Blinding. "Glad you're on board!"

He pumped my hand up and down. Did he say *Afghanistan*?

TUESDAY MORNING ROLLED

T uesday morning rolled around. I'd promised Nick I would report to the Office of International Programs, Foreign Posts Division first thing.

Would they put me on a plane immediately? To Afghanistan? I'd gotten a form letter welcoming me to the office and thanking me for taking the detail, but no other word from anybody...about anything.

Did I need shots? How was that ground conflict?

Also: Why the hell was the FDA opening a branch in Afghanistan?

I might have been out of the loop, socially and in sanity, but I'd checked out the clips every single day. Maybe after...after Elise and the kids—I wasn't conscious of what I was reading for the first few months? Hell, maybe even the whole year, but I would remember updates about opening a post in Afghanistan, about some breakthrough pharmaceutical or food or device development, or any activity at all. From *Afghanistan*.

Wouldn't I?

Then again, maybe not. What did I know about its current leadership? Nothing. How about that war, still going on? Did we still have troops there? No clue. If they'd hit it big in pacemaker manufacturing, I guess I wouldn't know that either.

I decided to go for a walk. To see Ravi.

The sun felt good on my scalp, actually. It had been a long time since I'd gone outside while the sun was up. It was kinda cool out, for early Summer. Maryland weather always keeps you guessing. In the old days, the campus used to be a wind tunnel in the Spring and turn into a scorching heatfest by now. But now there were all these ornamental trees to cool things down.

And a post in Afghanistan, for reasons unknown.

Was 66 the right one? I could have sworn that's what Ravi said. I swiped my card through the reader again and again, but for some reason I wasn't getting the green light.

I peered in through the glass panel in the door. Inside the lab, a lab I apparently wasn't qualified to access, Ravi sat hunched over...I don't know what. Could have been a glorified Brita water filter, same as I had in my refrigerator back home. But this one was hooked up to electrodes.

He noticed me lurking, smiled and waved. Sprang up from the bench to hip open the door, hands full of beakers. "How ya doing, buddy? Come on in."

"I'm alright. Thought I'd see what was so important they hid it in the basement."

"I know, right? Tunnels. Not just for storing office equipment anymore!"

Early in our careers, when we were fresh-faced—

I guess I should say, when *I* was fresh-faced. Ravi was still full of pep. Too much pep. How did he do it? I caught a glimpse of myself in a lab mirror and I didn't see anything that remotely resembled who I was ten years ago, five years ago. One year ago.

Early in our careers we explored the tunnels under the FDA in our spare time. It was mostly used to store office chairs back then. Now the chairs were gone, replaced with labs. Really high-tech labs. Apparently Ravi was leading one of them.

"Wow," I said. "You've done well."

"Yeah, right," he laughed. "This old place?"

Meanwhile, I'm still stuck in a mid-level analyst job in planning. Which tells you what a slacker and a loser I must be, because any white guy who showed up wearing a shirt and pants and not completely drooling on himself wound up managing some office eventually.

Not me.

"Nothing old about any of this," I said, and it was true. "What the hell is this thing?"

"It's for electrophoresis. We're separating molecules using an electric field. Helps with DNA and RNA analyses. That over there is a transilluminator. We use it to look at DNA that we've stained."

In the past year or five, I hadn't stained anything more than a shirt. Pair of pants, maybe. I stopped in front of a cage of two morbidly obese mice. "Looks like a tiny tanning bed. For these massive mice you've got here. What's wrong with these guys?"

"Wrong? Nothing's wrong. At all. Are you trying to body shame them?"

"Why? Can they understand what I'm saying? Are they geniuses? Did you teach them English?"

"I ought to. We call them the Americans."

"That's offensive," I said, patting my own drooping stomach. "They look nothing like me."

"The study is pretty cool, actually. We're studying a hormone that affects their insulin secretion *and* their cognitive abilities. GIP."

"I'm imagining that stands for something?" I tapped the cage. The mice didn't even stir. Barely even a look in my direction. Their huge little bodies were crushing their own rodent feet. There was a mouse wheel in there. Was that for irony?

"Spoken like a true FDA employee. You want all the acronyms spelled out up front for no reason. It stands for glucose-dependent insulinotropic polypeptide." Ravi shoed me away from the cage. "Stop it, man, you're stressing out my babies."

"So you're down here working on fat mice." I moved over to the Brita filter, and he ushered me away from that too.

"Not mice, *rats*. You'll never believe who's funding it. Go on. Guess. You want a coffee?"

"Uhhh, Department of Energy. No, I just had one."

"Terrible guess. What do they want with obesity drugs?"

"If they could figure out how to use this stored energy," I pointed at my gut, "We could solve the energy crisis."

"Cool concept," Ravi said. "But wrong. Try again."

I stroked a beard I didn't have. "Hmmm. Thinking, thinking. Department of Ag. Trying to head a food shortage off at the pass by figuring out why we're all eating so much."

"Not even close," Ravi shook his head, rattled around in a drawer. "I'm going to tell you because you're never, ever going to figure this one out." He pulled out a little piece of plastic.

"Hit me," I said. I pointed at the little dome in his hand. "What is that? You taking my DNA?"

He popped it in one of his many potential mutating devices and hit a button.

"Espresso," he said. The machine sputtered out the same. "You need to get out more."

"Right," I said.

"Joint funding," he started again. He pulled a carton of milk out of his genetic chiller and poured it into a stainless steel beaker.

"Looks like science, but it's a cup of coffee. I'm waiting," I said. "Me and the taxpayers."

"Everything is science, Jim," Ravi said. Then he lowered his voice. "The Department of Homeland Security and the CIA."

"Spies," I said. "These fatties are spies." I turned back to the fat mice. They didn't look like future spies.

"Spies, Jim. This is some fat espionage. Very low profile."

"As low as it gets," I said. "Basement level."

He stuck a wand in the beaker, and I watched him foam his own latte milk. "Hey, they're expensive," he said. "I wanna retire someday."

"Fat mouse espionage," I intoned.

"Very low profile *and* very high profile. Somebody from HFAC called me the other day."

"What is, High....Fructose..."

Ravi interrupted acronym Jeopardy with, "House Foreign Affairs Committee."

"Maybe they're scared that we can't run away from anything because we're too fat and out of shape."

"Don't shame yourself for being fluffy, Jim. Anyway, we'll never know. They pay me to do the experiments, not to ask why. And they're rats, Jim, not mice. It's fun work for me. Better than reading other people's clinical trials day in and day out. If I have to answer to some Senator, so be it."

"I thought you said it was the House calling."

"Yeah, that's what they said."

"Well, then it wouldn't be a Senator, would it?"

"I guess. I don't know how the government works."

"Who does?"

"Said he was a Senator though. Senator Tom Fletch. Senior. New Jersey. Called me right here. I don't think I've gotten a call at work in seven years. Republican, I think. Or maybe he said Democrat. Who cares? We're not a partisan Agency. Something for everybody to legislate here at the FDA. Maybe he didn't say." Ravi added the foam to the espresso, then elbowed me out of my rat eye contact until I acknowledged his latte art: an intricate series of three foam hearts. "Bet you wish you ordered one of these now, don't you?" He slurped the first heart down. "You wanna continue on the tour? We've got a whole room for CRISPR work, all the latest stuff in next-gen sequencing—"

"Actually, I wanted to tell you about something, get your take on it." There were a few lab techs swirling around in the cubicle forest just outside the lab. I didn't know if I should be talking about my future assignment out in the open or not. "How about we take a quick walk?"

"Sure. Sure thing." Ravi hung up his lab coat. I was sweating through my standard government-worker, cornflower-blue button-down shirt, and for no reason: it was kinda cold in there. We went topside and hit the path that wound through the double helix sculpture and around the back of the complex.

"Remember the last time we ran into each other, you said you'd heard I was posted overseas?"

"Yep."

"You were right. You knew it before I did. Nick Chang told me earlier this week, after I ran into you. They want me to go to Afghanistan with the Foreign Posts—open a branch office. I've hardly been...I'm not the obvious choice. Why me, why Afghanistan?"

"Oh, wow. You know—" Ravi dropped whatever he was going to say first, threw up his hands. "I don't know. They keep me in a basement. What do I know?"

"That's what people who know something say," I said.

"I have to report to our steering committee for this contract. I saw something about Afghanistan on an agenda for one of the quarter-lies. It was above my pay grade, I didn't attend."

"If Senators are calling you at work, maybe your pay grade is about to change," I said.

"Here's to hoping," Ravi said, and cheerlessly laughed. "Word on the street is, there's going to be some pharma activity in Afghanistan, or there already is. FDA needs to get ahead of it."

Ravi was on a different government street than I was, one where you hear words on it. A street on which Senators called you.

"Since when has FDA gotten ahead of anything? We're known for the opposite, aren't we? Not reacting to dead bodies. For years and years. Homeland Security is studying fat mice and now we're opening an FDA branch in Afghanistan? What's there to get ahead of, exactly? Sounds crazy."

"I'm not crazy." Elise was on the couch, fists clenched.

"I know you're not," I said. But my *tone* was wrong. I saw it immediately. When you're married you always have to get the tone right.

She'd been crying all afternoon. Now she was really wailing. I was worried Ally would wake up from her nap and join in with a wail of her own. Elise had been to nearly every kind of doctor there was. For two years. There was no medical reason for her to be in pain, and yet here we were.

"I have no idea," Ravi said. "Let me know when you find out."

6

A SEVEN-FOOT-HEAP OF

A seven-foot-heap of a federal investigator at the front of the room banged his slideshow clicker against the wall, a PowerPoint slide lighting the inside of one big red ear. I was two days and three hours in on a long, meandering series of presentations dedicated to teaching us about the FDA's Office of International Programs, Foreign Posts Division.

So far, I'd learned nothing.

"Alright, everybody. Let's get started again. Top ten most wanted. Here we go. Let's see if I can get the clicker to work. No, that's not it. Try this button."

What was the incentive for telling us about foreign criminals? Were they proposing I catch them?

In Afghanistan?

Me?

What about the overgrown mutant at the front of the room? *He* should be out there punching criminals in the face—not wasting his time trying to use a clicker.

He could have been an FDA experiment, too, just like the rats: What happens when you raise a baby straight out of the womb on nothing but human growth hormone and grass-fed beef? The audi-

ence looked more like me though, a federal employee leftovers semi-
nar: invite only, send your most broken. The woman next to me was
openly picking her nose. Not in a polite or delicate way.

Ring finger in. Knuckle-deep.

"There we go. Now we're cooking. Okay." A blurry picture of a guy
stared back at me, who, thanks to my astigmatism, looked exactly like
my next-door neighbor.

Brian.

"Dima Shevchenko. Born 1970. Ukraine. President of XoXoRx,
LLC—a fraudulent prescription drug distributor operating out of
New Jersey and Montana. Shevchenko and his partners acquired
discontinued, altered, counterfeit, and expired pharmaceutical drugs
that they then sold and distributed to drug wholesalers in Puerto
Rico. These wholesalers then sold and distributed the drugs to independent pharmacies here in the United States..."

Thanks, globalization.

Get my career hopping again in good old Afghanistan.

The linebacker up front, after a few tries, managed to click the
slides forward. He was learning. Maybe all you needed to thrive in
this world was to intimidate people with your physical presence and
to be able to advance PowerPoint slides.

I couldn't do either.

"Kwa Lele Odoki. Born 1980. Uganda. Leader of a terrorist group,
the WLA, created in part by siphoning off development funds and
arranging false erectile dysfunction pharmaceutical sales to the US,
for which she was arrested in Mali late last year. She evaded extradition and escaped. Operating out of Zambia now. Allegedly."

Kwa Lele had eyes that burned with a fire you didn't see around
these parts—at least, not in a crowd of federal employees. Any job
that involved determined foreign criminals wouldn't be for me. Or
any crime-committers at all, really.

Not even misdemeanors.

My stomach turned over.

I needed to talk to somebody about what a bad idea this was, to
transfer me to Afghanistan. Maybe I had nothing to lose in life, but I

hadn't gained anything that would tip my hand towards winning, either. Especially against criminal masterminds.

Maybe I wasn't up to working any job. But whatever it was, exactly, I sure as hell knew I wasn't up to working *this* job.

I LURKED by the reception desk. I'd been stalking Nick Chang without any luck all week. Mornings in a training in Rockville, afternoons stalking my boss back at White Oak. Cursing to myself in my car on the commute back and forth. That's what this week was so far.

"Jim, I need to talk to you." Jane Foxhall. "Got a second?" Rocking a pantsuit. Did she wear a pantsuit every day? I couldn't remember from the old days. I hadn't seen her since the holiday party three years ago, before Ally was born. She looked exactly the same.

I'd jumped a little, when she said my name. I hoped she didn't notice. A grimace on her face said she had.

Head of OIP. Lots of rings on her bureaucrat hands.

For Jane Foxhall, I had all the seconds in the world. Besides Nick, she was the only top-level monster inside the Office of Planning who might have the faintest idea why I should go to Afghanistan; what we were doing in Afghanistan; why I, of all people in this godforsaken building, would be qualified to do *anything*. Least of all, in Afghanistan.

"Of course," I said.

"Great. Let's head down for a coffee, shall we?"

Disappointing. If we were talking in public, whatever she was going to say to me couldn't have been that important. I wasn't going to get any real info, not in this meeting. Nothing critical was shared in a place without a door. Hell, they didn't even allow risky PowerPoints anymore, in case some assholes FOIAed us. And they always did.

One of my first assignments was to calculate the workhours behind all the citizen lawsuits.

One of my second assignments was to calculate the cost to taxpayers of all the *industry* lawsuits.

So you can see why I stayed for ten years. Exciting stuff, right?

Jane and I took the sixth-floor bridge. Down there in the cafeteria, all the tiny office workers were eating lunch. I followed the back of her pantsuit across the skywalk and headed down the staircase. Used to be regular old steps, plain and simple, some stained carpet from the eighties. Now it was a glass-and-steel number straight out of the Louvre.

Crack of thunder. A woman close to us screamed and dropped her cafeteria tray, broth and noodles splattered. The glass wall closest to us vibrated itself apart, millions of tiny pieces of glass on the carpet, in the broth and the noodles.

Not thunder. Louder.

Jane stumbled down the last couple of steps in her heels. I followed, already breathing hard.

"What was that?" I said. I took her arm, barely touched it on the elbow, really. She didn't exactly rip herself away, but she got out of reach quick. Real quick.

"Bastards," she mumbled. On the far side of the cafeteria, closest to the FDA main entrance, a crack in the other window spread from the center, travelled the full length of the pane. The window shattered in front of us, rained glass down on our shoulders. I looked outside, through the empty frame.

Building 66. Smoking.

You'd think in the United States we'd be clued in to the concept of a *second* incident.

A second boom. Floor surge.

This explosion dwarfed the first.

The collapse of the second tower, another explosion right after the first, second gunman on the grassy knoll, whole lot of other examples in there, I'm sure. Second World War. Second Gulf War. The next recession, the next collapse, the other shoe drops. We even have an old expression about it.

But I wasn't ready. The second explosion was a whole series, each louder than the first, now without that piece of glass to protect my sensitive ears.

I crouched down and clutched my head like they'd taught James to do in his lone gunman drills at school.

The floor vibrated underneath me and then stilled.

When I poked my head up, Jane Foxhall was standing there, upright and staring at me. Disgust, probably, but all her expressions looked exactly the same.

She didn't look like *she* perceived any danger, despite whatever the hell was going on.

"Lousy low-bid contractors," she said.

She looked like she *was* the danger.

"You get yourself to safety, Jim. Go lock down in your office. I'm sure it's just another demolition mistake."

"Oh—okay." I said. I stepped carefully, crunching glass under my loafers.

Jane Foxhall didn't give a shit about that explosion or anything else in this world. "I have to lead the emergency exit procedures," she said. "I'm the red hat for our office."

No, she wasn't. I'd seen the updated emergency contact list in the clips a month ago.

Jane turned and marched out in the direction of the blast, high heels on glass. That wasn't even the right way to go for emergency exit.

People were filing out of the cafeteria, some stoic, some concerned. I heard the punchline to an old contractor joke.

"I'm all for cutting corners on demo, but this is ridiculous." The security guard from gate D. One lady was crying, one of the older ones. She clutched her work badge and held it out in front of her like it was a shield. The Bell Curve of human emotions. I fell in line.

I took short breaths in the aftermath of smoke and debris. Out past the rat grasses, beyond the new molecule statues and the ornamental trees, a figure emerged. Just past the exploded wing. Briefcase tucked under his arm. Pivoted his head in all the directions, and then he bolted. Straight out into the woods.

It was Ravi.

7

THE NEXT DAY

The next day, all three buildings around the lab had been razed, and there was an email apologizing for a minor construction error.

The email announcement went on to explain it was all part of the planned building improvements, and that those employees had been relocated to Rockville as per the master consolidation plan. I wondered.

Did the Rockville relocation include Ravi, though, or was he still in the woods somewhere?

Contrary to her pearls, pantsuit, Jane Foxhall's office looked like a Caribbean cruise souvenir shop. I got distracted by a beach-scene coconut sculpture over her left shoulder, a montage of tropical vacation pictures.

"Sit down, Jim." People always said that to me. The weird part is, I feel like I usually am sitting down. You know, statistically. But whenever I'm not, somebody wants me to be. Anytime somebody has bad news to deliver, they always try to get you less vertical. I don't know where the tradition stems from. Maybe they don't want you to pass out and hit your head from shock.

Because that creates more trouble for *them*.

I sat down.

Sit down, Jim. Your wife, she was obviously deeply disturbed at the time of her death. But it wasn't her fault.

The implication: It was my fault. And it was. I should have been able to do something. I had all the power and proximity to save her and our babies from a completely avoidable death.

Will you still love me when my face starts to fall off?

Of course, Elise. Why? Are you expecting that any day now? Big laughter. Fake anger.

Kissing. Was that a false memory, the kissing? I can't remember anymore.

"Jim? I said, do you know anything about Afghanistan?"

Oh. Uh-oh.

As an average man, the reassuring thing about being around career federal employees is that, even though I know there's a fifty percent chance they've done a better job than me, they can't be that smart. I might be out of my depth most of the time but I'm not in here with coked-up hedge fund managers and 19-year-old Internet entrepreneurs. It's usually safe in here, from talent and ambition, and that feels really good.

I searched my brain.

"The Soviets invaded it for a decade starting in the eighties? Then the US sent troops in to get rid of the Taliban...or Al Qaeda? That was in 2001? Or two? I knew a few guys who served there over the years— my neighbor, an old classmate from high school. They didn't say much about it. I'm not too sure what happened lately—ISIS?"

I studied a pastel painting of a conch. This lady was going to eat me alive. I'm not international. Why would anybody volunteer me for an international post? I'm a local man, I feel comfortable saying and doing local things. Let's eat crabs, for Christ's sake. Talk about the Ravens.

"I'm not going to inform you on the security situation. You'll be in a training about it over the next few weeks. It's not our expectation you'll get involved in any political activity over there, anyway."

Oh, good. This wasn't a *diplomatic* mission.

"I called you in here so I can tell you what your job is."

The most direct, specific, and clear sentence I had ever heard a government supervisor utter. I stopped squirming and I leaned in. My neck was sweating.

The phone rang.

Jane Foxhall answered it. She looked at me. She held up a manicured finger. Her wrist bracelets clanked.

Another minute or two passed. She pointed at the door. She mouthed something, either, *I'll catch up with you later*, or, *go fuck yourself, moron*.

I saw myself out.

———————

A FORM EMAIL to greet me Thursday morning.

Congratulations, James Schreiber! Your detail to the Office of International Programs, Foreign Posts Division has been approved.

Your start date is June 7. Period of service is 90 days.

Was I going to Afghanistan for 90 days? On Monday?

I flung open my office door and walked right into Deputy Director Nicholas Chang's surprised face. Really nailed him. Chest-to-chest contact. We recovered as awkwardly as two grown men who never meant to touch each other could.

"Sorry, Nick. I was just coming to see you about this form letter I got. Am I going to Afghanistan on *Monday*?"

"Right—OIP told me you'd be getting notice. You're not leaving for four more weeks, that's what I was coming to tell you." He had to do his glasses ritual now that I had run into his chest. Eyeglasses off, chamois out of pocket.

"Great. Because. I don't even know what I'm doing there yet. I mean. Are there any...shots?"

"Vaccinations?"

No, I mean *gun*shots. Am I gonna get shot in the face?

"Good question. I don't think so—no malaria in the desert, right?

Maybe Hep A, update your tetanus, though. When's the last time you travelled?"

Never.

"I was on a cruise once. You didn't need shots."

"You'll learn about it at the State Department. You're scheduled for a training there starting tomorrow. They'll tell you everything you need to know."

"Okay."

"You can take the shuttle from here or report downtown directly to State. The main building over on C Street. It's a two-week training, Jane told me. We'll see you when you get back."

Nick was name-dropping Jane Foxhall now. He must be looking for the Director promotion. Poor Nick would never ascend, even with those sparkling eyeglasses. His decrepit corpse of a boss would be reanimated before he ever allowed Nick to take his place. He came to work about once a month, said the opposite of what he'd said on his previous visit, slighted Nick, and that was that. Nothing to complain about. At least he was consistent.

———————

THE STATE DEPARTMENT smelled like mold.

"You've got three options: Run. Hide. Fight. If you can get out, get out. If you're stuck in there and you're already in his line of sight—and I say *him* because we've not had any female active shooters yet—your best method of survival is to work together. Throw something, distract him, then swarm him. I'm going to show you a short video now to demonstrate."

Our representative from security dimmed the lights. On the screen, an actor playing an active shooter forced the government worker extras onto the ground and pretended to shoot them in their heads.

If an active shooter could even get in here, he deserved some kind of award. I'd circled the building three times before I could find any entrance. Then it took me another 30 minutes on top of that to get into the training center.

"I don't think I'm in the right training," I said to the guy next to me. He looked like he was 12 years old. "I'm not a new employee."

"No? Returned? Contractor?"

"No, no. I'm with the FDA."

"Where you going? China?"

That would make sense, wouldn't it?

"No, Afghanistan. We're opening a branch in Afghanistan. So they sent me here for foreign service training." I'd gone from pretending this was classified information to blabbing it to any child who would listen to me in a matter of weeks.

"Oh. Hmm. There's a post for ya. What a shitshow, huh? Just another Benghazi waiting to happen. Good luck. You're in the wrong training. Foreign service class is down the hall."

"Damn it. Okay, thanks."

I snuck out the back while the fictional gunman shot a woman cowering in her cubicle. Should have fought back, lady. You could have thrown your stapler, *then* gotten shot in the face.

Shitshow? Benghazi? What was the child employee talking about?

I should have stayed and asked him. I would have learned more than wandering the halls of the State Department, alone and lost. Four labyrinthine hallways later, I'd passed three eagle statues and an eagle painting and I still couldn't find the damn foreign service officer training.

If I could ever find the exit, I was going to go back to the FDA and tell Jane Foxhall, Nick Chang, and anybody else responsible for this stupid decision to call it off.

I GLOWERED in my office for the rest of the week instead of tracking down Jane Foxhall or Nick Chang. My interactions with other people needed to take baby steps in these initial stages of rejoining the sphere of humans who spoke to each other—no matter how sparsely that happened in government. Except for automated responses like, "Excuse me" and "Thank you," I couldn't think of much that I'd said to anybody after the funeral. I had to really gear up for key conversations, like ones in which I refused to go Afghanistan to open a branch of the FDA unless I got some real answers about what a *Benghazi* was and how it was going to apply to me.

I flew into Building 32 bright and early Monday morning, so intent upon getting answers for myself that I forgot to neglect the hall of medical malpractice.

While I waited in line for security to verify my badge and admit me into the ID-scanning turnstiles, I came face to face with the very safe and very effective synthetic surgical grade Gynsecur®-brand pelvic mesh, medical device number 929327591, new and improved over its predecessor, Polymesh®-brand pelvic mesh, sitting next to it, the most porous chastity belt in all the Middle Ages. I'd been avoiding it for a year.

Sit down, Jim. I know this is a difficult time for your family, but it's best if we do this now—name the cause of death.

It's not a difficult time for my family. They're dead.

I sat down and crossed my arms. I stared past his face, observing each of his eight medical degrees and certifications.

You said Elise had complained about some stomach and back pain. How long had that been going on?

The doctor was about the same age as me. Ring on his finger. Wouldn't have ignored his wife's pain.

Elise in the bathtub for 36 minutes, Allyson screaming from her crib, James stomping animal crackers into the carpet: that never would have happened to him.

Jim, I think something's wrong. Maybe you should go to the doctor, not let's go to the doctor or I'll take you to see the doctor or let's make an appointment to go to the doctor.

Clutching her stomach in front of the mirror. "I'm not getting my body back the way I did last time." Oh Elise, you're just being hard on yourself again. You look great.

"My back hurts." There's ibuprofen in the cabinet.

"My pelvis hurts." There's aspirin in the drawer.

"My stomach hurts." Want some Pepto Bismol?

"I think I'm bleeding more than usual this month." Are you sure? Blood always looks like a lot more when it's outside the body, doesn't it?

"For some time," I said. "What are you getting at?"

The doctor shifted in his seat, adjusted his watch.

"We think this incident stemmed from an operation she had following the birth of your second child."

Allyson's newborn screaming followed by Elise's adult screaming.

Is this normal?

I wanted to scream too.

"Her uterus collapsed before she could pass the placenta. She's going septic. We have to sedate her and do a reconstructive surgery." The nurse shoved me out of the way.

They carried Allyson away, slimy and shrieking. I didn't see where she went. And I couldn't wait for Elise to wake up. I needed her to wake up.

Elise did wake up. She did. And when she did, she had a brand new vaginal floor of her own, held together with synthetic surgical grade Polymesh®-brand pelvic mesh. Hell, they didn't even number devices back then. Side effects include vaginal bleeding, abnormal discharge, dyspareunia or vaginal pain. Psychosis. Painful voiding, urinary frequency, urgency, hematuria, recurrent urinary tract infection, urinary calculi, and urinary fistula.

FDA stepped in eventually, but it was mostly up to the civil suits to incentivize that crippling chicken wire off the market.

Not enough adverse events to trigger a recall.

8

MORNING COFFEE BREAK

Morning coffee break. The break should have been from thinking obsessively while doing less than nothing about my current, info-deplete situation. Instead I brought those obsessive thoughts with me on an unfocused stroll to the coffee shop in Building 11.

Maybe it was doing something for me, to be around people again. To leave my office during daylight hours. To hold myself upright and see other humans, could there be a benefit in that?

"Jim? Jim!" Ravi, from somewhere behind me, off to the left. I had been drifting down the main corridor of Building 1, near the plastic men wall art. From far away it looked like something medical, something you would expect at the FDA—molecules, or a virus, or DNA. When you got closer, you saw it was thousands and thousands of plastic men of various colors. All of them fluorescent.

I stopped and turned. I must have had a look on me. Ravi's face was concerned. I'd been reminiscing too much.

"Hey! How ya been?"

I hadn't been fleeing the scene of an explosion, that was for damn sure.

"Okay," I said. "I heard you got relocated to Rockville."

"Yeah."

"Did all those rats survive the...construction accident?"

He smiled, kept glassy in the eyes.

"Yeah," he said. "They all made it, thanks. I wanted to continue our conversation from the other day. Do you have time?"

Only another day or two.

"Sure," I checked my watch to seem like I was together, busy, mentally fit. I followed Ravi's shoes outside. High-tech, swoopier than the usual shoe, better design. Like you'd see at Google, I bet.

We wound our way down the path and sat ourselves down on a series of concrete slabs between Buildings 22 and 1. It was too cold to be outside sans coat.

But the trip to get it wasn't worth missing out on what Ravi had to say.

"I'm glad I ran into you," he said.

"Me too," I said.

His phone vibrated. Loud. From the front blazer pocket.

He jumped off the concrete slab—really threw himself into it, too, like somebody had stabbed him in the back. Struggled with his fancy jacket, made a big show of checking the phone to see who it was.

But you could tell he already knew who it was, by the way he jumped off that slab.

"I'm sorry," he said. "I gotta take this."

"No prob," I said.

"I'll catch up with you later," he said. He slid his earbuds in and my info session evaporated.

Fine, Ravi. My stomach hurt anyway. Better to head back to my office, drink some Pepto Bismol.

I LINGERED outside the regulatory failures exhibit after lunch in the cafeteria, alone, turkey sandwich, staring session: the three building-sized pits in the ground.

My trainings were complete. And the paperwork was done. There was nothing left to do.

Except for somebody to tell me why the hell I would be going to Afghanistan.

And then, to go. I still didn't know whether I would do it or not.

I peered in the glass case, at the mesh that sliced through Elise's organs sitting next to the mesh that healthfully, helpfully propped up women's collapsed vaginal floors. How many notices had the FDA ignored from hospitals and doctors?

Ignoring things. Me too. At the time, I was just trying to get through it. I hadn't delved, then or now. Only ignored.

A shadow inserted itself between me and the glass case.

Jane Foxhall.

"Walk with me, Jim," she said.

So I did.

"The past is behind us," she said.

It wasn't, though, not for me. Not the least little bit.

Heels falling, echoing until we reached the broken hallway with the plywood instead of glass. "We need to fail forward."

Fail forward? Was that the latest? What a stupid government catchphrase.

"It doesn't do any good to live in the past," she said. "For regulatory bodies." She stopped walking. I stopped walking too. "Or for people."

I nodded. My auto-response.

"This work in Afghanistan? It's the future."

"The future," I echoed. I recalled a song from the late nineties, Holler Back, Girl. I think that's what it was called. It went something like:

I need to holler back, girl. I need to holler back, girl.

Jane forced the issue. "Well? Have you decided?"

I couldn't live the second half of my life the same way I lived the first.

"Yeah," I said. "I have."

9

NO MATTER HOW

No matter how much I jiggled the latch on my airplane food tray, it wouldn't hold. One more thing to crush my legs besides a seating design that eliminated foot room and my own bad packing job. Now that eating time was over, I had nothing to do.

Last leg of the trip: Dubai to Kabul. I wanted to do something besides fidget, but I hadn't planned for it. There weren't even any prep files. In the X-Files, Mulder and Scully always had some pre-investigation material, something to go on.

I shouldn't have based my career in public service on the idea that I'd one day investigate aliens.

I'd downloaded the Pimsleur Beginners Arabic and listened to the first lesson last night, when I couldn't sleep because of my sheer terror. I tried my new skills out on my Afghan seatmate.

"Marhabaan," I mumbled, what I hoped was the correct pronunciation. That got minimal response—a half-nod, part shrug. Maybe he wasn't even from Afghanistan.

Without any in-flight entertainment, I was stuck. I did have one piece of instructional paper, so I decided to read it again. I strained hard to reach my second carry-on, down by my feet, and my back seized up. Not meant to be. I gave up.

When I woke up, I was blinded by sunlight that could only have been more intense if I had landed on the actual sun. My seatmate was gone, without even so much as a tap on the shoulder to rouse me. The last stragglers were leaving.

"Wait! I'm here!" I yanked my bag up and stumbled out of the plane, into the makeshift corridor. Then I remembered my informational piece of paper. Hadn't it said something about this? I rummaged through my carry-on, back straight, so as to not agitate the growing twinge of seizing pain. But there was no loose sheet of paper in there anymore. One critical piece of paper and I'd already lost it. Light shot through the cracks in the corridor, laser beamed all around me.

Did I still have my diplomatic passport? I tapped inside my shirt, next to my wildly out of control heart rate. Yeah. Still there. Still an American citizen. I wasn't signed up for an entire life in Afghanistan. I could figure this out without my piece of paper.

I kept going, towards the light. The corridor opened up into the tiniest representation of an airport terminal I'd ever seen, of the four I'd seen. Recognizable equipment—a conveyor belt, a....wait a second. Had I left my other bag on the plane?

Yep. I'd packed four bags—two to check, one for my foot area, and one above me. I'd left my backpack in the overhead on the goddamn plane. The doors to the plane were closed behind me already. Two men with guns in front. Rushing towards men with guns and screaming in English wasn't going to do me any favors.

Shit.

What was in that bag? My Arabic phrasebook, some clothes. A picture of Elise and the kids.

It was so bright, I couldn't think. My mouth was dry. I was panting. By the time I hobbled through my what-was-in-that-bag thought exercise, our bags started coming out at the baggage claim. Unlike at Dulles or BWI, the Afghans got everything done in this one room.

The other passengers picked up their bags, one by one, and

brought them to an x-ray to be scanned. I followed the others. Something in my stomach pitched around at the thought of going outside. I had only a few recalled images of Afghanistan in my head—all from the third Rambo movie. I thought I had maxed my heart rate in getting off the plane, but no.

It would be so embarrassing if I died of a heart attack at the Kabul International Airport.

Well, boys, it looks like this middle-aged man was murdered by the mere *concept* of danger.

I took a step towards the exit.

"Sir! Sir!"

I turned, with dread. It had to be for me. Nobody else in the terminal had responded to words spoken in English.

It was the flight attendant, running towards me with my forgotten backpack. I took a deep breath. Things were going to be okay.

"Thank you," I said. I bowed a little, in case she didn't understand. She nodded. She did understand.

Afghanistan probably wasn't even that explosive anymore. The Afghans would look after me. An official-looking guy stamped my passport and that was that—I was in.

The next issue was Afghanistan cash, how to get it. The terminal was sparsely decorated...sans food court, ATM, merchandising, or Smart Carte® to transport my bags. Would the taxi accept American dollars? I walked outside and beheld the most elderly fleet of Toyota Corollas.

"Taxi, sir?"

"I need to change some money. Is there—"

"Yes, yes. Right this way." A young man grabbed my suitcases before I agreed, and led me down a path farther away from the safety of the terminal.

Here we go. The kidnapping begins.

We reached a guy with a card table, plastic chair. Stacks and stacks of money. Colorful. Soon I had a stack of local currency of my own fattening my money belt under my shirt, and we set out for the

United States Embassy Compound in a Toyota Corolla from the nineties.

So far, so good. Didn't work exactly like things in America, but I was getting around alright. Maybe the news was just hype.

The streets were thick with dust, cratered, lined with barbed wire. Several kinds, from what I was seeing. Slabs of concrete poked up everywhere for no good reason. But it was fine. Peaceful. No explosions.

"Here it is," my young taxi driver pulled over by the side of the curb. I couldn't see anything except glare and concrete. "That will be ten thousand, nine hundred, and twenty Afghani."

The money was called the same as the people.

"Gosh," I pulled out my stack of Afghani. "That seems steep."

"This is...conversion. Afghan money is worth nothing."

"Do you tip in Afghanistan?"

"Not much, but if service is good—"

"Well, here you go. Let's round that up to eleven thousand."

"So generous. Thank you so much, sir. Very, very generous, the people of the United States, all the time. We are so fortunate to have you here for many years. Many, many, many years. We hope for so many more."

"Say, where is the compound?"

"We are here." My driver pointed out the window, but all I saw was a massive concrete wall.

"Right. I know you said that, but I don't see anything."

"I am not able to drive any closer. The guards will shoot us. But you may walk under the wall here, go to...ah, second gate, and guards look at your passport. Then you are outside your United States Embassy. I have never been inside. My cousin went last year. He tried for a visa."

"Did he get it?"

"No."

"Sorry to hear."

"Is okay. No problem. He is a terrorist."

"Ha ha. That's not a nice thing to say about your cousin."

"It is true. If you give him a gun and small salary, he will shoot anybody you say to him. One day he is Taliban, then Al Qaeda, then ISIS, now Syria."

"That's a shame."

He shrugged. "Economy is not very good in Afghanistan."

"Can I ask you one more question before I go?"

"Yes sir."

"Am I saying this right...Marhabaan!" I shouted it a little. I don't know why—I always did that when I tried learning Spanish, too, for a cruise Elise and I took to Mexico before the kids were born. *Donde está la playa!* I shouted everything.

"Yes, sir. 'Hello.' Very good."

"Okay. Great. So, people in Afghanistan will understand when I say that?"

"Yes, sir. Many Arabs visit Afghanistan, so we understand their language. We speak many languages here for the visitors: English, Farsi, Arabic, Hindi, Chinese—"

"Wait. What?"

"We speak many—"

"Are you saying you don't speak Arabic here?"

"No, sir. We are not Arabs. We are Afghans."

"You don't speak Arabic?"

"In Afghanistan we speak Dari, Pashto, Tajiki...many languages."

"Oh." Why did I think they spoke Arabic? I thought that with so much confidence I didn't even Google my way into accurate information.

My new Afghan friend helped me wrestle all my bags out of the Corolla and onto the curb. Then he got back in and drove away. I was all alone in Kabul, out in the open, in front of a concrete monolith.

I got dizzy after a few steps and had to set down my four-bag luggage configuration, look down away from the sun, catch my breath. I had been outside for 30 seconds and I was already getting sunstroke. No wonder nobody could ever conquer Afghanistan. I used up the last of my bottled water from the flight. My heart was pounding. Out in the desert with no water. Recipe for death.

Nobody to help me, nobody in sight—the embassy street was silent. This was no...what? New York City? Cabo San Lucas? I had nothing to compare this to except one Mexico cruise. Okay. Keep going.

I pulled myself and my bags together, and after twenty minutes of plodding I finally found an opening in the concrete where I could file in and face another concrete wall, some more barbed wire, and when all the barriers opened up, down the road—what looked like it might be a security station. Preventing access to the United States Embassy Compound.

Almost there. Don't die outside now.

Two beefy men with guns and a guy inside a one-window shed appraised me.

"ID?" I slid my passport through the tiniest little passport-sized slot in a thick, thick window.

"Where the hell'd you come from? What's in these bags?" Two of the hugest men I'd ever seen congregated beyond the turnstile. Their guns weren't pointed *at* me, but they weren't pointed *away* from me, either.

"Uh, it's my luggage. I just got here. From America. Washington. DC. I'm a new...employee?"

It sounded like a terrorist cover story to me, too. I didn't have any papers or orders or letters of introduction—I'd had one instructional piece of paper that I'd lost. It struck me again what an ill-conceived job transition this was turning out to be, from start to finish. These guys were going to shoot me right in my dumb face.

The guard inside the shed called out the back to his turnstile-protecting associates: "Hey! It's Jim Schneider!" He stepped out of the shed and waved my American passport like it was the flag.

"Oh shit," the guy on the left said. "It's Jim Schneider. Jim Schneider! What the hell are you doing out there? Get in here!"

"You're in trouble, man." the guy on the right said. "Whole compound been looking for ya. We all placed bets!"

I saw a green light flash on the turnstile, but the boys had already grabbed me and my luggage and started muscling me through.

"What?" The light and the turnstile operability weren't connected. I could have walked through at any time.

"You're the first government employee to roll through Kabul without a gun and a bunch of other men with guns around you. In 18 months! Jim *Fucking* Schneider. We thought you ran out into the desert and joined ISIS."

"But I just got here. What was I supposed to do?"

"All United States federal employees make a hard left when they get off the plane, Jim. It should be in your welcome documents. We never go through the terminal. Certain death in there. He winked. "How the hell did you get here?"

"I took a taxi—"

"He took a fucking taxi. I'll be damned. What the hell am I holding this piece for, wearing all this Kevlar?" He threw his hands in the air and it jostled a few guns strapped to him. I ducked. I wasn't used to being around weapons. "It's Disneyland out there. I knew it."

"We had an armored car waiting for you on the tarmac for an hour. Eleven people showed up, the twelfth went AWOL. Our man Jim. Where'd ya go, we all wondered. Is he nailing hookers in Dubai?" The light was so bright. Their voices were getting farther and farther away.

"I'm sorry. I lost my welcome paper. I...I think I'm going to pass out—"

I finally had some street cred for the first time in my life and I was going to lose it to dehydration.

"Okay, Ironman. Have a seat."

My massive, deadly welcoming committee shoved me into a plastic folding chair behind the shed. One of them ran away and returned with a bottle of water. I blacked out. When I woke up, still upright, at least, the water was running down my scalp. It all seemed like a dream anyway, being in Afghanistan. The two soldiers had, like, military onesies on...on top of that they were wearing vests and other vests and additional straps with guns in them, and they were carrying guns on their backs—I had sweat completely through my short-sleeved polo shirt.

These guys were cheerful. In that heat. With that amount of clothing. Unbelievable.

"I don't know what's wrong with me. I don't have asthma or anything, but I can't breathe."

Why was I here? I didn't have any babies anymore. That was why I'd been selected: our designated FDA representative. Not Leslie. Not Stephen. Not Deputy Director Nicholas Chang. Not Jane Foxhall.

"That's altitude." He pulled another water out from one of 86 or 87 utility pockets and handed it to me. "You ever been to Denver? Mile high? We're higher up than that. You gotta drink a lot of water and take it easy the first week. You'll acclimate by week two or so. I'll call a cart to come pick you up. You were supposed to come in on a helicopter, not trot through town like you own the place. Did you know that?"

"No, I didn't. I'm sorry if I caused any trouble."

"No trouble now that we found ya with all your limbs still on. I lost twenty bucks though. I figured you turned scared in Dubai, then high-tailed it back to wherever you came from."

"Not yet." I poured some more water on my head. It wasn't cold anymore but it still felt good.

"Welcome to Afghanistan."

"Thanks," I said. "I don't really know what I'm doing here."

"It's okay," he said. "Nobody does. Drink more water."

10

LET'S GET STARTED

"Let's get started. Come on in, everybody. If you haven't gotten your picture taken yet, you can get it afterwards. Which brings me to my first topic. Advance the slide, please. Bob, could you hit the—?

When I say advance slide, you go ahead and...yeah it's the button on the right. Left. I meant, left. It's the button on the left, Bob. No, not that one. Just—I'll come show you."

Twenty of us gathered in the auditorium for the intro security briefing. Eighteen men. Two ladies. I wondered about the profile of people who got selected to come to Afghanistan. Maybe every one of us had been widowed already. Afghan and American flags popped up on the screen, and then a slide that said, *Pictures*.

"As I was saying, I'm John Warfield. This is my eighteenth stint here in Afghanistan. I've retired six times already. They keep dragging me right on back. Probably do the same to you."

He pointed at me.

"I love the pay, and I love the food. DFAC food is the best food on earth. Don't let anybody else tell you different." He winked. That was the second or third wink I'd seen in two days. Why was everybody so flirtatious here?

"If you get a suspicious looking package, they're gonna call me up —no matter what time it is. If it's time for Thanksgiving dinner. Then I'm gonna put on my bomb suit and go investigate that package. Even if it's cookies from your dear Aunt Sally, we're gonna blow it up. Blow that sucker right up with the robot if we can't identify it. Me and Billy over there are your bomb squad."

Billy waved from the sidelines. Billy was a little vacant in the eyes. John Warfield looked like the real deal—the kind of guy I would expect in Afghanistan. Old. Grizzled. Alert. Like he'd been blown up a few times and then sewn back together with extra nooks and crannies in his face. Man's man. Didn't struggle to change a tire.

"This picture you starred in over here for your base PIT-card, that may be the last picture you take...until you all get home safely and go back to your Facebooks and your Snapchats and your Instagrams and your selfies. With the exception of Anne's Courtyard, you can't take pictures anywhere on the compound."

"What's a PIT-card?" I hissed to the guy next to me. He shrugged. Nobody knew anything. The presentation featured a bunch of inexplicable and unspecified acronyms that reinforced how little we all knew.

"That includes pictures of your Afghan colleagues. They don't need you advertising them on the Internet. Next! Next, Bob. There we go. Thanks. Helicopters. You all came in on one. Almost all of you. Isn't that right Jim Schneider. You troublemaker."

John Warfield stared at me until my face throbbed red. I hoped it wasn't noticeable beneath the blistering sunburn I'd suffered earlier. I'd never be able to work with a bunch of badasses. Give me back my federal bunch of eye contact-avoiding misfits with zero confrontation and butter-soft hands, please.

"*Most* of you came in on one. You'll all be leaving on one. Let's talk about helicopter safety. You wear a hat on that helicopter, it'll be your last hat and your last helicopter. When that hat gets up in the rotors, you and your fellow passengers will crash and it'll be all your fault. Hats are a no."

I loved hats. I would have killed us all. It's just as well I took the taxi.

"Open-toed shoes are not recommended. And, if you're drunk, you're not getting on my helicopter. We'll send you back to the compound. You can sleep it off and join us for another beautiful day in Afghanistan. Next."

"IEDs. Improvised Explosive Devices. If you're out rolling through town, and you hear a metallic clink on the side of your door, you're gonna wanna get out of that car. That's a magnetized IED. Of course, they'll shoot at you when you get out. They might not be great marksmen, though. Maybe you'll be able to crawl away to safety before you get shot or that car blows up. Next."

Four Afghan men crouched near a massive hole.

"This crater here is from a VBIED—a vehicle-based IED. They packed a 1993 Toyota Corolla with a few tons of explosives, drove it up here and parked her outside the gate, and that's what it looked like after. Here are a few slides to show you what they look like, so you can try running away when you see one."

I recalled the details of my ride through town and I felt faint.

"We can't play the sirens for you today because there's a top-level briefing going on next door, but we test the emergency system every Friday morning at 5 am, so you'll hear what that sounds like tomorrow. When you get into your housing—whether that's a wet CHU, a dry CHU, or one of these fancy apartments we've got now—you're gonna wanna try on your protective gear. You all should have a helmet and a flak jacket somewhere on the premises. Make sure it fits. Maybe the guy before you was six foot nine, I don't know—better to get yourself squared away before you need it."

I couldn't listen anymore. I was going to throw up. I stared at the floor. When I looked up, a woman across the aisle from me averted her eyes and turned her head—a moment too late to stay undiscovered. She looked a little bit familiar, but that was impossible. Who the hell would I know in Afghanistan? Either I recognized her from the hallway of fifteen minutes ago or I was having a stroke. Too much excitement already.

11

TIME FOR DINNER

T ime for dinner at the DFAC: 6 pm.

Department of...Food....Access? Nah. If it was intuitive, that wasn't it. I couldn't recall any translation from the many, many orientations and tours. It *was* the place to get food. I knew that much. I set out from my CHU very slowly, shuffling from foot to foot, then stopping when short of breath.

Was it possible to *never* adjust to altitude?

I thought I had made it to the DFAC, though every building looked about the same to me. Sand colored. Moderately hideous in the United States Government fashion. No labels or defining features. Instructions to get from one point to the next were complicated and based on an intrinsic personal knowledge: for example, turn left at the gazebo where we all smoke our cigars on Sunday afternoons.

The men breezing by me on their way to dinner or who knows what were mostly spitting images of my welcoming committee from earlier—huge men carrying huge guns. Visible tattoos. Visible muscles. Every now and again somebody slightly different would come along, a real standout...the out of shape, the elderly, the woman.

I was being approached by a composite of the latter now.

"You must be Jim Schneider! Thanks for taking the time to meet with us on your very first day in town, Jim. I'm Paul. Paul Tussey." I shook hands with Paul, Paul Tussey. Despite his portly physique, Paul breathed and moved like a Russian ballet dancer—perfectly acclimated to the altitude. He wasn't even sweating even though it was about a hundred degrees out there, and he was wearing a ridiculous 26-piece suit ensemble. Still scorching at 6 pm. I turned to the old woman. You could tell by her demeanor she was the kind of old woman who didn't think of herself as an old woman.

"Polly Dolius. Great to finally meet you, Jim. I'm with USAID and Paul here is with State. But let's talk inside, out of the sun. Have you eaten over at the East DFAC yet?"

By the time I was done shaking Polly's hand, my eyes were about to roll into the back of my head. I hadn't followed their titles or their career paths or whatever she had started to tell me.

No, I haven't eaten at the East DFAC yet, Polly. I'm barely getting by. I don't understand how you're doing it, walking and talking at your advanced age, here inside this furnace.

"No," I said. "I don't think so. It's been kinda a blur."

It wasn't the comforting swamp-like heat and humidity of northern Maryland that I was used to—it was this dry, piercing burn all around you and with too much sun to boot. It didn't matter what kind of clothes I wore. I was burning alive in the sun every moment I was outside.

It was obvious why nobody ever conquered Afghanistan.

I followed Paul and Polly's backs and tried to make appropriate responses to their chatter. I felt a little bit better once we got through the security checkpoint, better still at the hand washing station, and by the time we'd had our meal cards scanned and I was appraising the DFAC buffet, I thought I might live another day after all.

"Did they set you up with the standard plan?" Paul asked.

"I don't know," I said.

"Well, let's ask. We don't want you to go hungry."

He chatted with a lady of indecipherable origin at the register who'd swiped my card. Hairnet, uniform. Same McDonald's-style protocol as any other American food establishment. Paul handed my card back to me and our hands brushed a little. His was warm and dry compared to my sweaty mess. I suffered a wave of nausea at the contact for no real reason.

"Eligible for three meals," he said. "You eat what you want while there, take two to-go boxes with you if so desired. You can scan in for two daily snacks on top of that."

"I guess I won't starve," I said.

He pointed down a side corridor. Polly was up ahead, already three food stations-deep in the buffet. "Coffee is freely available around the clock—I suppose to keep our guards from sleeping on the job. Nice change from domestic federal service."

"Sure," I said. "I'll save a lot of money on lattes."

"Oh. Lattes aren't included," he said. "But there are plenty of options around for you to spend the big coffee bucks. Three, I believe. And if these food options aren't enough, there are four additional convenience stores, two bodegas, and five or six little restaurants scattered around, plus a late-night pizza option...all the comforts of home."

But in Kabul.

I grabbed a tray and a plate and peered into a sidelined buffet of, potentially, a chicken dish and stewed potatoes, puffy bread, a few unidentifiable sauces.

"This is food they make for the Gurkhas," Polly heaped some on her plate. "Try it sometime. It's pretty good." I'd tried enough new things for one day, or year, but I wanted to humor my new colleagues, so I dabbed a little bit of something yellow onto my plate.

It wasn't a big place, the DFAC. There were, what, 50 people? Not to mention everybody hiding in their CHUs, eating alone. All I'd really learned so far was that everything had an acronym here: my food, my temporary home, and the bombs people would use to try and blow me up.

"How many people are here?" I fumbled open my plasticware set, unraveled my thin paper napkin and put it in my lap. Elise would have been proud of me. Or my mom. I was blanking now on which one of them trained me to do that. My dead mom or my dead wife.

"On the compound?" Paul was halfway through his plate already. He wasn't a shy eater. "Thirteen hundred on this side. Then you've got NATO ops on the other side. ISAF claims they're not active anymore but there's some movement over there, and they can be bothered to help us out from time to time on crop eradication. We still sit in on meetings."

"You came at *precisely* the right time," Polly cracked open an unidentifiable can and took a sip. At least I knew ahead of time it wasn't Arabic written on the side of it there—then I would have really been an embarrassment. I had an Afghan taxi ride to thank for saving the tiniest bit of face. I wondered what the Afghan language was called. Had the driver told me? Was it called Afghan? Like the people and the money?

"The eradication's gone well," Paul said, forking a heaped scoop of macaroni and cheese off his plate. "Despite what you might have seen on social media—that field of poppies they posted wasn't even current."

"It was stock footage they found in the archives. Can you imagine?" Polly snorted and swigged her not-Coca Cola again.

I hadn't seen a damn thing on social media. How did this elderly lady even know what social media was?

"Do you speak any Dari, Jim?" Paul put a valiant effort in with his plastic knife, carving up something advertised on the buffet labels as mutton.

What is mutton, anyway? Sounds so medieval.

Dari.

"Not yet, but I'm hoping to learn quick. Then I'll be able to read what that soda is." I gestured at Polly's drink.

"I'm sure you won't have any trouble," Polly patted my arm. Was she patronizing me? "But this is *Arabic*. They import this one from Dubai."

She *was* patronizing me.

"Anyway, now that D4D is in full swing—it's a cooperative agreement, not run through the G2G—though we did address it at the PSE summit late last year, it's really opened the floodgates. We've got every big pharma corp in the world banging down our door. They can't wait to partner." Polly shoveled in some more Gurkha food. My eyes drifted to a television behind her: the weather report for all US military bases in the South Pacfiic.

"Really remarkable stuff," Paul chewed. "I don't think we've seen a program with this much potential in decades. Other parts of the USG have been studying the rare earth deposits since 2006, and you know China's had an agreement down in Helmand as long, if not longer, but this—" Paul raised his eyebrows.

"We've still got some trouble with the cartels and the land rights to work out, but we're about to get even more support on that, and now that we've got your FDA expertise in-country..." Polly trailed off.

She and Paul exchanged glances, glances I couldn't interpret. Something about the meal reminded me faintly of the feast scene in Indiana Jones and the Temple of Doom. I don't know what, though. It's not like Paul slit open his one big macaroni and cheese to reveal a messy mass of smaller macaroni and cheeses bursting out and slithering around on the plate. Suddenly I felt sick. Too much G2G and D4D talk. Hurt my head. My heart. And my stomach.

"I'm sorry," I stood up. "It's been such a long day. I think I need to turn in now."

"Oh, look—there's Diane. She's with the DEA. I think she came in with you today. Let me introduce the two of you." Polly waved.

I whirled to spot the lady who avoided eye contact with me in the security briefing earlier—the vaguely familiar one, the one who looked at me like I was the ritualistic human sacrifice: put me in the cage, tear out my heart, lower me into the flaming pit.

"I have to go," I said to Polly. "We'll have to meet another time." I couldn't catch my breath, and I was dizzy again.

I bulldozed my way through the dining hall, nearly bounced off a security hulk and the guy in charge of the dessert booth. I broke into a near-trot trying to make it to the trash can to dump my tray and get the hell out of there. Instead of sliding it into the opening, I crashed it

into the side of the can. Hard. Gurkha yellow sauce splattered my
shirt. My plasticware was down on the floor. My drink was down
there too.

And then Diane was upon me. I sensed Paul and Polly glaring
from my abandoned table.

"Hi...Jim, is it?"

"Hi Diane. I've gotta go. Can we do this tomorrow?" I didn't wait
for an answer. I got the hell out of there. I'd met enough people for
one day.

12

A MOMENT BEFORE

A moment before dawn. Even with only a hint of the sunlight to come that day, everything was illuminated. That never happened in Maryland.

I was late.

I ran from my CHU, letting the door snap shut so hard it rattled the CHUs around me. I sidestepped a newly-reshaped part of the sidewalk, skirted the DFAC—no time for breakfast today—and took the pedestrian tunnel that ran you east-west. I flipped my badge up at the guards to get out of holding and into the *heli* area.

"Jim Schneider?" Big guy with a clipboard stood in front of a few different helicopter diagrams that showed me the areas around each helicopter model in which I might be beheaded. Either that, or the areas where I was safe.

"Yes." I was hopeful for a security briefing to describe which situation the diagrams portrayed.

"Right this way."

No security briefing.

He led me through a set of leaden doors and onto a scruffy open air yardage where only the weeds were doing great. This must have been the soccer field, as everybody called it. Today it was the helicopter landing field. He still hadn't told me which helicopter I'd be using that day so I trailed way, way behind to avoid missteps, beheadings.

I couldn't hear anything above the thwacka thwacka of the chopper, there and ready to either behead me or depart with me in tow. Big guy with a clipboard gestured me on. I nodded too vigorously. I climbed the ramp, where another big guy—my chauffeur, it seemed, thrust a heavy package into my hands and gestured: *Put it on, stupid.* My Personal Protective Equipment: PPE. Similar suit as in my CHU. I'd tried it on after orientation, after John Warfield had suggested we all try ours on or potentially die later. Didn't seem life saving. But then, I guess you never know what the cocktail of ingredients will be in your continued life versus death. Who could say what a weighted vest paired with a visibility-ruining helmet could do for me when this helicopter crashed? I struggled them on.

As I knew from my initial security briefing, if I'd been wearing a hat, we could have died. So I was *sans* cap. Open-toed shoes were counter-recommended but not deadly. I'd already learned so much in Afghanistan: that I never wanted to travel in a helicopter, and I didn't want to leave the base.

My chauffeur wrapped a cable into a tidy coil and settled himself at a large gun pointed at the ground outside.

Today I was going to do both. Before sunup.

We lifted.

The next stage in my arrival to Kabul, after my airport misstep, my security briefing, and my lousy dinner meeting, had been a series of awkward meetings with various representatives across the federal government—even a few from the Afghan government. One after another they tried to tell me what my job there was, exactly, and meeting by meeting I continued to understand next to nothing.

Here's what I did know.

1. They'd discovered some rare earth minerals in Afghanistan
2. These rare earth minerals were used in pharmaceuticals

3. My job was to assist a point-of-site manufacturing and quality inspection operation for the pharmaceutical processing

4. I was completely unqualified to engage in any of this but for some reason the vague and near-worthless skills of *management and program analyst* were considered sufficient in this case

Finally, in disgust, Polly and Paul—Pauly, in my mind, they'd popped up together so many times—ordered me out to the job site. FDA's new office location. This was my punishment for not knowing any of the acronyms or the context and being a poor altitude adjuster and a poor sport—they were sending me out into the field. Alone.

Probably, to die.

Touchdown.

"Jim!" I was watching a touchdown, Super Bowl whatever, some team that always got to the Super Bowl versus some wild card who never got to the Super Bowl. I'd bought myself an even bigger television the week before and it looked fantastic. More high def than high def, somehow. God that was a great TV. Elise was tending to the kids upstairs. She hollered at me about something; I ignored it.

It was a commercial. They're the best part.

The helicopter touched down so gently I could almost ignore it, and I tried to, until the big guy who handled the cables and the gun looked at me, expecting.

"Where are we?" The rotors died while I was in mid-shout.

"New Kabul. Your stop."

"Where's Old Kabul?"

"Old Kabul is just Kabul."

"Aren't you coming out with me?" He motioned for me to return my metal hat and flak jacket. My only protection.

"Nah, you're first on our list, we're backed up all day. We'll pick you up as soon as Artie calls it in."

"Artie?"

"Artie. With MRI."

"NRI?"

"MRI. You always get on a chopper without knowing where you're going and who you're gonna see?"

"This is my first one. I don't know what I always do on them." I reluctantly dragged my protective vest over my head until my thinning hair stood on end. I flattened it with my sweaty palms.

"Alright, then. See you later, Jim."

I peered out the back ramp they'd lowered to reveal a trailer and a small hut that fit the bill for site of my future murder.

"You're not coming with me? To do...introductions?"

"No, sir. We've got a lot of pickups today," he flicked his clipboard, "And you're delaying them all right now." The pilot started the rotor again.

They meant to leave me here in the middle of nowhere. Allegedly with a man named Artie—and Artie was nowhere to be seen. There was nothing else around for miles, as far as I could tell. Not much visible on the way in, except a bit of the ground from underneath my helmet, out the window, peeking out past the gun, which took up most of the good window space.

I edged out. My complicit murderer waved me away from the helicopter.

If I got beheaded by the helicopter, I couldn't get beheaded by anyone else, and that would ruin everyone's fun.

I scurried away, dirt kicking up around me, whipping my chinos and polo shirt. I should have tried to get some clothes that blended me in more. I don't know what. Like sand-colored robes, or something. Whatever they wore around New Kabul. Then I could lie on down there and hide from view while the sun killed me.

I shouldered my backpack and walked up to the buildings.

I had a few viable options, none of them fantastic:

1. poke my head in the mud hut.
2. poke my head in the trailer.
3. wander around out there until I inevitably stepped on an IED and blew off a leg, then drag myself to either the mud

hut or the trailer—or lay there and bleed out without doing any additional work.

I decided on option b.

I baby stepped over there as if I'd already entered the minefield, like the security video had shown me. I didn't have a pocketknife on me to dig around in front like you were supposed to if you thought you'd stumbled onto a minefield, so the whole thing was a real crapshoot anyway. I was banking on the helicopter guys *not* touching down in a place that would have directly endangered me, then taking off.

Safe bet? I didn't know.

I rapped on the trailer door. No answer. It wasn't big enough *not* to hear a knock. I knocked louder.

Was that a sound?

I gently turned the doorknob, a gleaming hot fireball already at 6 am. I peered in, but my eyes couldn't adjust fast enough. Rapid shuffling inside.

"Some old man got jumped right outside my house. I live in Silver Spring, not Compton. Sheesh."

Some old man looked up at me from his cell phone.

"Can I come in?"

"My wife had to go help him look for his dentures in our shrubs. It's not right. America's down the tubes."

"That's terrible, uh...Artie?"

"Once you hit a certain age, I guess you have to buy a gun. Then when dementia hits, everyone's screwed." Artie threw his phone down and looked at it like it had jumped an old man too. Then he glanced up at me. "What are you waiting for, an engraved invitation?"

"Uh, yeah, I guess I was." I edged into a trailer crammed with loose papers, some ramshackle office equipment, a cot. The Afghanistan version of the Unabomber's cabin in the woods. Smelled like burnt coffee and rancid mayo in there.

"Jim Schneider, Artie Halboch. Nice to meet you."

"Likewise," I pumped his dry husk of a hand up and down, and I decided to level with him.

"Artie," I set down my backpack and took out a bottle of water. "I gotta tell you the truth. I don't even really know why I'm here."

"All I know is, the Taliban was destroying all those poppy fields until the United States invaded. After that, heroin got cheap as hell, stock market went booming, and people started overdosing all over the damn place."

"What?"

"Just kidding! I'll show you why you're here. Come this way." Artie pulled out a faded and ancient ruin of a baseball cap that barely announced MRI and pulled it low on his head.

"What's MRI?"

"Contractor. Me, contractor. *I'm* MRI. You, government."

"Just you?"

"Some other guys, too. As needed. Stands for Mining Resource, Internatiônalè."

"Oh, so it's not American?"

"No, it's American."

"Internatiônalè?"

"I think they made a mistake when they were incorporating."

"Pretty big mistake. Get a whole word wrong."

"I dunno. Maybe it's easier to fuck up a river in a made-up language and get away with it."

"Did they?"

"Fuck up a river?"

"Yeah."

"Yeah. Eighteen times, per the lawsuits. Internatiônalè isn't even a real word in any language."

"What do you do?"

"I manage the job sites. Logistics, stuff like that."

"I see," I nodded.

He shoved past a few piles of paper that threatened to tip, shut off the burned-up coffee pot, and led me out a back door.

I followed Artie's back through the searing sunlight, down a path, around a hill, where we came upon a steep concrete staircase that might have been poured last week.

He stopped short.

I did too.

At the edge of the largest, deepest pit in the earth.

The temperature dropped, and all the places on my body where the sweat ran, which was *all* the places on my body, my skin ran cold.

"Jim, meet Mineral X." I heard the wind whistle from deep underneath, where it was too dark to see. "Mineral X, meet Jim." On the sides of the manmade canyon, the dirt ran a shade of red I'd never seen before. I felt my heart pounding in my stomach. I was breathing through my clenched teeth like I was back in Elise's Lamaze class. "Take 'er easy there, buddy!" Artie clapped me on the shoulder. "This little pit ain't gonna kill ya."

I wasn't so sure. I didn't feel well, I still wasn't breathing right, and whatever I was looking at, it seemed out of place on Earth and out of bounds for a lowly office worker—the pit *and* the red dirt *and* the unexplained glow at the bottom. I didn't see my spreadsheet skills applying here, not at all.

13

AIN'T NO PARTY

"Ain't no party like a Kabul party."

"Oh." I jumped, only slightly. I was becoming a real people person. "Hello, Diane."

"Hi, Jim. I see you didn't get the memo."

Diane looked like a ghost, with her ashy skin in her lacy white tank top and flowing white skirt. Two hundred or so of our colleagues were wearing less ghastly ensembles of the same color.

Apparently the French embassy down the street was having a big soiree, but only a handful of Americans could attend due to the security concerns of shuttling vulnerable members of the invading force down the street at this hour. Not to be outdone or out-partied, we were compensating, like this: A *white* party.

And boy, was it white.

"I didn't research the party attire requirements before I packed." I was wearing a blue button-down and khakis. Middle-aged desk jockey or consumer electronics repairman uniform. We crowded onto the balcony behind the West DFAC, overlooking...I didn't know what. A big, dark warehouse? I hadn't been doing much exploration around the compound since my first week. Mineral X, site A was taking up all my time. Just a few trips over to the ISAF side to eat Thai food for the past few weeks; besides that, I only had the energy for work and sleep.

"Jello shots! Shots! Shots! Shots shots shots!" A hulk with an ornately sculpted beard heaved a microwave box in my direction. I reached in and grabbed a Jello shot for myself plus one for Diane.

"Pretty classy around here, huh?" Diane squeezed her Jello shot into her mouth. I tried to do the same, and failed, dug it out with my finger. When was the last time I'd done a Jello shot? Never? When's the last time I did any shot? College.

I wasn't much of a party guy then, either. I hated screaming over the music. I wasn't a good dancer—no rhythm. I wasn't a great small talker and nothing's changed. Elise saved me from years of looking dumb and out of place at parties when she took me off the market just beyond my twenty-first birthday.

Would she do it all over again, knowing the outcome? The answer had to be no. There was no woman in the world who would choose what happened to Elise.

"I said, how's it going with everything?" Diane screamed into my ear. The crowd around us waved their hands in the air like they just didn't care, prompted by the music, and vocally emphasized by our DJ.

"It's *fine*. It's going *well*." I spied Pauly over by the drinks table. They looked like they were having a heated argument. More likely just trying to get a conversation in over the music.

"A match made in hell?" Diane shouted.

"No, I said it's going well!" I couldn't scream any louder than I already was. The music cut out in time for me to shout that over the crowd. Nobody cared. They were invested in drinking. I caught the eye of Paul. Polly daubed at a splash of beer on her white getup—t-shirt and Bermuda shorts. He elbowed Polly and gestured towards me.

"I know what you said. I meant them," Diane controlled her volume but kept audible. "Big Soviet pharma, US government edition."

"Yo yo yo!" The DJ boomed. Microphone feedback tore a groan or two from the audience. "We want to get this party started, right?"

"Right!" One or two of the crowd roused their own enthusiasm for call-and-response.

"Me too. But there's been a suspicious package sighting at the east entrance. Everybody dance your way to the exit in a single file using the staircase on the west side. West siiiide!" The DJ threw up a gang sign from the music videos of my suburban youth.

A few of the couples who'd been dirty dancing a moment ago groaned. One lady booed. Everybody else took it in stride.

"Ain't no party like a Kabul party," Diane looped her arm through mine. "Let's get out of here. Quick, before they catch up." She flicked her eyes towards Pauly.

We strode a sufficient distance away from either the bomb *or* the forgotten backpack—whichever it was, then into the compound's newest apartment complex: Diane's quarters, home to anybody stuck (assigned, *assigned*) for a year or more. Luxury compared to the lousy CHU I called home. We flashed our identification cards and the Gurkha security team nodded us through.

"Have you seen the library yet?" Diane punched the elevator button before I could respond. "It's small but respectable. We can have a chat there."

I heaved an internal sigh of relief. I had a lot on my mind with Mineral X, our new hire— Rahim, getting the inspections set up. Or making sure he did. I didn't want to see the interior of Diane's apartment today.

Not that I wouldn't consider seeing it *someday*.

Just not today.

I CAUGHT a glimpse of us in a mirror on the far wall. Diane and I looked like absolute ghouls. The library was small, and its lighting was garish—par for the course in any government building.

The duck-and-cover alarm had woken the compound up a couple

of nights ago. I'd stumbled into my pants, and then they cancelled the damn thing before I could even drag the body armor and helmet out of my standard-issue wardrobe. I'd yanked the pants off and climbed into bed. Then they'd sounded the alarm again: Get out of bed, get the pants on. Cancelled. Again.

I decided to blame that night's woes for my face looking like it was sliding off my head and down to the ground. Plus, the food. The food wasn't doing anything for me either. There was something about the institutional pecan pie that called my name every single night.

I eyeballed the library shelves, a lengthy collection of espionage paperbacks, but Diane wasn't here to wander and had already sat down. Ready. She was antsy now that we were alone. Was this a social call after all? My stomach started to throb. I went and joined her. No sense in delaying the inevitable. Whatever that was.

"You've seen Mineral X?"

"Yep. Met Artie. Saw it. Creepy looking."

"Do you know what it is?"

"No. Do you?"

"A little. I'm going to tell you what I know."

"Company policy?"

"No. The DEA doesn't give a shit about you. This is my policy."

We stared at each other while she waited for me to say something. I didn't know what to say, so she continued, saving us both from my low-reaction blankness.

"It's a weight loss drug."

"Like fen-phen? Blows a hole through your heart?" Weight loss. Ravi's research. Fat rats, meet Mineral X. Blows a hole through your heart; blows up labs, too? I never saw Ravi again after the blast, before I left for Afghanistan. Never got a chance to ask him what happened that day.

Diane smiled, but the smile didn't reach her crow's feet. I imagined she was sizing up my own growing paunch, swelling with daily pecan pie. She was right: I could use a weight loss drug too.

"No, not like that. It *works*. It's not any weight loss drug. It's *the* weight loss drug. And more. It's a cure-all. It's a goddamned miracle."

"You don't sound like somebody who's witnessed a miracle."

The emergency siren went off.

"Oh, shit," I said. "They know you're trying to tell me something classified."

Diane didn't laugh. "Let's go," she said. "In case it's some kind of Benghazi thing going on up there."

We took the stairs in case the building was already on fire, bombed, on the way to total obliteration. Or somebody microwaved the popcorn for too long. Could be either. I followed Diane's lacy white tank top and drooped upper arms out of the basement library and into the courtyard.

We stood around with a few dozen other bored looking bureaucrats in various states of dress and undress.

"No sign of a Benghazi thing," I said. Since arrival, I'd learned this referred to the slaughter of several Americans in a complicated event at the Libyan embassy. Not very comforting as an adjective.

"No. Doesn't seem so." Diane's voice deflated. Maybe she *wanted* to be attacked. Hell, what did I know about her? Who takes a job in Afghanistan? Then the real reason for the deflation revealed itself.

"Diane!" The Paul half of Paul and Polly, waving from across the courtyard.

"Get outta here," Diane said. "Save yourself."

I didn't argue. I beat it back to my CHU. Mineral X gossip would have to wait.

14

THE CHANGES TO

The changes to our worksite were obvious as soon as I climbed out of the chopper. We were turning into a regular trailer park out here, two months almost to the day since the first day. Our new FDA office trailer had been dropped off over the weekend, logo and all, equidistant to the abandoned hut and the MRI trailer.

Abandoned—hell, maybe whoever built that tiny dirt hut up on the hill was away on vacation, scheduled to return at any moment.

There was a lumpy bit on top of the hut: a poorly grown mushroom. Were the mud hut builders the first to discover Mineral X?

I escaped the heat to burst in on a heated debate between Rahim and Artie. I could tell it had already been in progress for quite some time by the pervasiveness of the burnt-up coffee pot stink.

"This is too much for profit." Rahim pointed at an open binder on our cluttered communal table. Rahim had been managing local operations for a month now, running from site A to site B, doing interviews, getting our future inspection team together, putting them all through the vetting process so we had the necessary paperwork in hand to prove they weren't terrorists: everything we needed before the mining operation showed up and started pulling that junk out of the ground.

"I think what you mean to say is, there is no God but Allah, and Mohammed is his *prophet*." Artie looked at me and rolled his eyes. I went and busied myself with the coffee pot.

"No. That is not what I mean to say."

"I know why you're upset."

"It is nothing about Islam."

"It's because we're infidels and we aren't following Islamic banking laws."

Rahim's eyes looked like they were going to pop out of his head. "Infidel. Infidel? The only infidel in here is me, for agreeing to do the work with you."

"Tell you what, Rahim. How about this. The training program is cancelled. We're not using any students at all. Contractors only. MRI provides."

Rahim didn't answer. He looked into his tea.

"I must travel to site B now." Rahim pulled a long overcoat off the coat rack, even though according to my sweat glands it was sweltering outside. "May we finish this conversation later?"

"Rahim, consider it already finished."

Rahim looked at Artie like he was being sent out to a firing squad. He collected a few papers from the table, pulled a dusty clipboard off the shelf, and held the spring-loaded door as it closed, so it didn't slam shut behind him. Maybe he *was* being sent out to a firing squad. I had no idea what site B was like. It was way over on the other side of New Kabul. Since I had been coming here, I had only helicoptered in and out on site A.

I'd only learned about site B late last week from Rahim. And *I* was supposed to be *his* boss.

"He saw the cost estimates from the statement of work." Artie threw some more grounds into the coffeemaker to start the coffee burning process all over again.

"And?"

"His idea was to use students. Locals. Afghan college kids. Fine.

Fine by me. Guess what? We didn't plan to pay them a whole hell of a lot."

"Is that all?"

"Is that all? I don't know what's *all*. He says he's having some trouble with the cartel. I don't know what that means. *Some* trouble. Who are they, anyway? We'll never know the truth. Did a neighbor throw a brick through his window? Boo *hoo*. Just some Afghan Al Pacino, face down in a pile of poppy."

Artie made everybody around us out to be a terrorist or a devout Muslim. So far I hadn't seen evidence of either.

"Why don't we see if we can't get them more money?"

"Maybe Rahim *is* the cartel, ever think of that?"

I hadn't. But I'd only recently started sitting around in this trailer, day in and day out. Artie had been here for months. Years, maybe, I didn't know when he'd started working for MRI. He'd had a lot of time to think things that could have been true or not.

"How long have you been here?"

"That's none of your goddamn business."

"Well. Maybe we can pay *him* more. Rahim. Through the FDA, I mean. Promote him."

"Maybe you can. I don't know what you can do. You're the mighty, mighty United States Government."

"You're in a real fit today, you know that?"

"My wife's on my back about the bathroom reno again. Why are we constantly fixing up a house we barely use?"

"*You* barely use it. She uses it."

"She got to you too, huh?" Artie shook his head and poured himself another cup of coffee early on in the coffee-making process, interrupting the flow. I sorted through the offensive cost estimate, trying to find what had disturbed Rahim. It was obvious right away: a series of zeroes by the hourly wages of our proposed inspection students, a single digit USD for Rahim's hourly wage, and there was Artie's massive salary on the next line.

"Christ, Artie. Don't you think we should pay them *something*?" I knew how much Artie made, more or less, but it was still shocking to see next to Rahim's pathetic little amount, all those zeroes.

"Hey, listen to me. You think an education in FDA inspections is going to be worthless here?"

"No, but—"

Artie slammed his coffee cup down.

"But *what*? I interned when I was a student. Made a bunch of dumb mistakes that cost my dad's company thousands. Unpaid labor is what kids are for, Jim."

"Maybe don't leave the cost estimates around then."

"Sure thing, boss." Artie yanked the binder out of my hands, snapped it shut, and threw it up on a shelf. "Thanks for the tip," he winked at me.

So many grown men had winked at me in the past two months, *I'd* grown to severely hate winking since coming to Afghanistan.

"I was serious, though. Whole argument is moot. We're cancelling the student program."

"Under what authority?"

"Anti-Terrorist Act. How about that authority? It's not worth the risk." Artie put his feet up on the desk. I liked him less now.

15

THURSDAY AFTERNOON, NEARLY

Thursday afternoon, nearly time to knock off. Usually an early end to the day on Thursday. Friday was our day off. Everybody's day off in Afghanistan.

I was trying to make sense of the proposed extraction schedule, line up the volume with the inspections on the spreadsheet.

There was a loud rap on my trailer's siding, right next to my head. Three times.

"I'm out!" Artie yelled from outside. "See ya Saturday." Perpetrator heard but not seen.

"See ya Saturday," I called through the vinyl.

Since Artie and I had gotten separate trailers, it was a lot more peaceful around the job site. Separation was key to a lot of relationships.

I toiled at the spreadsheet for another twenty minutes. The extraction schedule was so aggressive. No matter how many inspectors Artie brought in through MRI, we still couldn't pull off that kind of volume.

A respectful knock at my front door. Barely audible above my AC.

"Come in," I said.

"As-Salaam-Alaikum."

"Wa-Alaikum-Salaam."

"Good afternoon, Mr. Jim."

"Afternoon, Rahim. How are you?"

"I am well, and how are you?"

"I'm doing alright. How's your family?"

I'd learned after weeks of working with Rahim, my first Afghan contact besides my taxi ride on the way in, that Afghan society mandated no less than three inquiries into your health and well-being, and that of your family, if you had one. Otherwise you were being rude.

I was trying to correct myself. The openers were both in Arabic, too, which vindicated my preconceived notion that everybody in Afghanistan spoke Arabic. Win-win. I felt smarter *and* more adapted. And it seemed to make Rahim happy.

"Please, sit down," I said. I gestured at my as-yet unused chair for visitors. "Would you like some tea?" Also, in order to grease the wheels of productivity, I'd learned, you had to have tea around at all times and always offer it no matter what.

"No, thank you," he said. "I just had one with Mr. Artie." He and Artie were getting along better since their series of disagreements about every component of every single thing we were undertaking there: the schedule of extraction, who should do the inspections, how long it would take, how much money people ought to get paid. Rahim lost every single argument, of course, even though it was his country.

I didn't know if they were getting along better, actually. I'd started avoiding them instead.

Rahim didn't sit down. He leaned on the back of the chair with both hands. "I have an invitation," he said.

"An invitation?"

"For you."

"For me?"

"From my wife and children. They want you to come for dinner."

"Sure, I'd be honored." I didn't know if my stomach could handle food that wasn't DFAC-produced, didn't include pecan pie. I suppose if I prepped for it, I could try.

"Shall we leave now?"

"Oh. You mean, today?"

"Yes. Right now."

"Oh, well I—I was just..." I searched inside my spreadsheet for some way to get out of it.

"My wife has been cooking all day. The children are so excited to meet you."

The advance warning was very one-sided. I decided not to point that out.

"Uh. Okay. Sounds great."

I GROANED and creaked and moaned my way down to the floor while Rahim's whole family laughed openly at me until they cried. Rahim's wife wiped away her tears with her hijab.

"Oh, that's good comedy," she said.

"Happy to entertain you," I said. I meant it sarcastically, and I was only saying it to have a reply, fill up some verbal space. Then I surprised myself when it was the truth.

I was happy.

Rahim's youngest daughter tugged on her mother's housecoat until she stopped chopping vegetables and leaned over. She cupped her tiny hand over where her mom's ear must have been and whispered through the fabric.

Kids of that age were big on secrecy, I remembered. James had gone through it too. Ally hadn't been old enough yet to keep secrets.

"She has something she wants to give you," Rahim's wife said. I realized I didn't even know her name, because Rahim always called her 'my wife,' and I was too embarrassed to ask now. I'd have to ask him later.

"Sure," I said.

She walked over shyly, stopping a couple of times along the way to observe me and look back at her mom. When she got to me, she left a flower about a foot away, and then fled down the hall.

"It's a heather she picked on our walk today," Rahim said.

"She must really like you," Rahim's wife said. "She never acknowledges our family or friends."

"I picked up the flower and sniffed it. "How do you say thank you?" I asked them.

"Tashakor," Rahim said.

"Tashakor!" I called down the hall.

Everybody giggled again, plus a tiny giggle from down the hallway.

"Shall we take our tea outside?" Rahim asked.

"Alright," I agreed. Rahim and I took cups of tea out back, into his garden.

"Rahim, do you ever mentally chafe against the boundaries of your own life?"

"Do I ever mental what?"

"Chafe? Do you know chafe? It's when two things rub together."

"Like sticks? To make a fire? No. We have propane and matches."

"No, it's not like you're purposefully rubbing one thing against another. It's an accident. It's like, your thighs. Did you ever run or walk a long distance and your thighs rubbed together and it made a painful blister."

I could tell by the look on Rahim's face that had never happened to him and he was disgusted by even the mention.

"I dunno. Maybe it's a western thing. Sometimes you get fed up with everything."

"Fed. Up?"

Yet another phrase in my daily vernacular that translated poorly.

"Like, you've had enough and you get frustrated. Angry. Sad."

"Like when a member of your family dies?"

"No," I said. "Not then. That's different. *Fed up* is reserved for less sad things. It happens when you get cut off in traffic, or when you get a surcharge on a bill for nothing in particular but it would be more of a hassle to call and talk about it than to pay it. If you get a bad review at work, but it's because your boss wants to further his own dumb career and not related to your actual performance, which really did happen to be bad but the two are totally disconnected from each other in cause and effect."

"Sounds like a lot of chafing."

"It gives you this feeling, like worms in your brain. Like there's no reason or point to anything."

"My father had his house blown up three times. There was no reason."

"Do you think he mentally chafed against the boundaries of his own life?"

"No, But he did beat us a lot."

"That's terrible."

"Not really. We usually deserved it." Rahim sipped his tea. I tried mine, and it surprised me by not being that bad. Usually I didn't like tea all that much. Dirty leaf water. I was always more of a coffee person.

"Mr. Jim, what if one mineral could cure osteoporosis, pancreatic cancer, and epilepsy? Stop Alzheimers. Resolve all diabetes types."

"I don't know, Rahim, I'd say that's a miracle drug."

"And we are blessed to have this miracle in Afghanistan."

"Mineral X. People say a lot of things about it."

"Those things are true. And we need a miracle in Afghanistan. We do. All I ask is that we get to share in its benefit."

I knew there had to be an ulterior motive. I had eaten eighteen different things over the course of that dinner. It was a bribe dinner, it had to be. Rahim wanted something.

"It sounds reasonable to me," I said, and I meant it.

"Good," Rahim said. "Then you'll approve the inspections training."

"I—I don't know that I have that kind of....we'd need to vet the inspectors-"

Rahim smiled. "Perfect. I knew you would approve. I invited them here tonight, so you can vet them immediately."

16

WE JUST WANT

"We just want a seat at the table."

Rahim had driven us to a cafe downtown, next to the Apple store, where we could smoke hookah and drink tea, with a gang of children, who could corner me and guilt me into giving them jobs.

"We don't even want that," one of the older boys said. "We just want to be near the table and feed off the—" He turned to his friend and made a hand gesture, flicked his fingers at the floor, feeding an invisible animal.

"Scraps," his friend said.

Their third associate kept a grim stare, said nothing. Took a long drag on his cigarette.

"What do you want?"

I'd never felt more uncomfortable in my life than in the handful of times I was exposed to teenagers.

"We want opportunity. We know they sent you to make a center so that Americans can come and work here. All we want is to be able to work here too."

Even Afghan teenagers knew more about this project than I did. I didn't know if that was true or not. It didn't seem like something we would do: make a deal with the government, import our own workers. If I knew anything about the United States, and I thought I did, we'd take advantage of free or nearly free labor provided by a steady stream of locals for as long as possible. It didn't make any sense for Artie to stonewall this.

And yet he was.

Just looking to get this crap out of the ground as fast as possible, as cheap as possible.

Rahim breathed a cloud of smoke into the air and offered me the pipe.

"Apple flavor," he said.

"No, thanks," I said. "I don't smoke."

Could I help these boys?

Probably not. But for some reason, I decided to try.

"See, Mr. Jim? We're not terrorists."

"I know you're not, Rahim. That's not the—okay," I said.

The kid closest to me cracked a smile.

"I'll look into it," I said. I heaved a big sigh so they knew exactly how much faith I had in this process, in my ability to deliver. "Maybe we can have a scholarship program."

"How about a training program *and* a scholarship program?" The smoker said.

"How about you quit smoking these cancer sticks?" I said. That sounded like a nice, solid, dad thing to say. "What's your name?" I asked. He had longish hair, wore jeans that were slightly bell-bottomed. Could have tried out for a 1950s Beatles ripoff band.

"Daud," he said.

"You want a training program, Daud?"

"I do, yes. We see foreigners come and foreigners go. But this is our home. We need jobs. I want to learn something from you."

"Okay, Daud," I said. "Fair enough."

The other two exchanged looks. Hope. Suspicion? Nope. They broke out laughing, high fived.

"I'll get you a training program," I said. Foreigners full of empty promises. Were they used to it by now?

"And a scholarship program," Daud said. "Don't forget."

The fourth boy smiled, slow and controlled. He was the only one who hadn't westernized his clothes yet.

"Try," I corrected. "I'll try to get you a training program. And a scholarship program."

What the hell was I doing, *trying* to run for Mayor of Kabul? I couldn't get anybody a training program or a scholarship program if my life depended on it.

"No promises," I said, though we all knew I just had.

17

I SAW IT

"**I** saw it on the recording, Artie. A woman."

"Is she yours?" He fake-laugh spit-sprayed all over the table.

Here we go. I breathed in as much trailer HVAC as I could handle.

"What do you mean, is she mine? You think I'm letting a bunch of strangers onto the site?"

I was. I'd approved an entire inspections program over at Site B.

And I hadn't broken the news to Artie yet.

"I know you want to let all these terrorists in. Maybe you invited some hookers, too. Hell," he stabbed his index finger in my direction, "I don't know anything about you, Jimbo." Arched one unruly white eyebrow. "Maybe you're a straight-up freak." He jabbed the air again.

"That's cute, Artie. Real cute." My face was red hot, I could feel it. This always happened when I was angry, stuffing it deep into parts of my body, where later on it could explode with cancer. My face skin was such a traitor. Looked so guilty, there was no incentive to not be guilty.

I moused the cursor over and clicked *play*.

A slim figure crept in from the shadows on the right side of the screen. Looked around in all directions. Stumbled a little, then corrected. Crouched down, out of video shot. Stood up. Looked around again. Hoofed it out of there.

Our camera technology wasn't the best, but you could tell it was a woman. Dressed in western clothes, scarf wrapped around her head and face.

The headscarf, in this case, was a disguise, not a tradition. It was obvious, and I never would have believed you could tell this kind of thing about a person from a distant and blurred recording, but her *movements* were western, too. Jangly. Looked American. Reminded me of Diane.

"THEY'RE in bed with the Russians," Diane said.

"Who?"

I was in bed with Diane.

"Paul and Polly. They have been for years. Hell, maybe they are Russians. They stand to make a lot of money off Mineral X. I'm sure of it."

"That's quite a conspiracy theory you've got there. Is that DEA-funded research?"

Every other visit to her apartment reeked of sewage, and this was one of those times.

"It's not a conspiracy, Jim, and it's not a theory. Check out all the cables on the high side, you'll see it all. Forty years of this. Cold War business as usual for Russia. They got rid of their nukes, okay, you win this time, USA, pivoted their whole operation. Played the long game."

"What's the long game?"

"Biomedical terrorism. Attack the food supply. Get BPA into everything. Make everybody chronically ill with the deadliest long-term combination of food chemicals and endocrine disruptors ever conceived, accidentally or not. This one, *not*. Bury all the evidence by funding contrary studies and fueling false clinical trials."

Diane was lightly pushing on my head, trying to make me less than level with her, horizontally.

"Everybody games clinical trials though," I said. "It's not a—an act of *war*."

"During World War II, there were hundreds of Nazis working covertly in the American government, totally undetected. Would you call *that* an act of war?"

"Nazis?"

"Yes, Nazis. They stayed undercover and reproduced in-country. Living inside our borders. Fathers working for the State Department. Raising little Nazi sons who grew up to work for the State Department. Still going on today. Nothing's changed."

I couldn't dispute what Diane was saying. I typically spent my Sundays watching pro sports. Diane obviously spent hers researching Nazis.

And, quick FDA question: Why *was* BPA in *everything* in the United States, nowhere else? She was right about that. I only knew so because I'd worked on the legislative rule analysis; it wouldn't cost suppliers anything to switch out the can linings. Receipt paper. Food packaging. Several hundred other products that caused irreversible genetic damage. Potentially. I mean, potentially *enough* that it had been banned the world over.

But not in the United States of America. A very influential BPA lobby made sure of that.

I edged my way down to the foot of the bed. These sheets were like burlap. Standard issue, US Government sheets. Probably had BPA in them.

One country in the whole world where an endocrine-disrupting, obesity-causing food storage lining was legal. Just commerce. Right? Profit. Not espionage. Certainly not biomedical *terrorism*.

"Russians," I said out loud. Now I was just buying myself time.

"And they're not even the real threat." Diane nudged my face closer to her pussy with the back of her calf. Pussy. Listen to me. I was like a rapper now. Elise never would have tolerated that kind of language. Hated that word.

"Who's the *real* threat?"

"The fucking *Swedes*," Diane said. And I couldn't even check her face to see if she was serious, because she'd taken both hands and plunged my own face way, way in there. I had a theory of my own by now: Diane was the woman in yesterday's recording. She'd trespassed at Site A. Why? I'd thought I would ask her on this visit, *yeah right*, but now my mouth was full.

Clever move on her part. Diane wasn't dumb.

18

ARTIE FARTED A

Artie farted a low, loud, squishy *thwacka thwacka*.

"God *damn* it, Artie," I slammed down the coffee pot and fled to the far side of his trailer.

"We're not married, Jim. I don't have to impress you."

While I was hiding over there, I sorted through the mineral purity inspections paperwork.

His system was, he had no system. So it was slow going. The perfectly mimicked smell of rotting fish inside a sulfur mine ultimately hit my nose anyway, despite the distance.

"Artie, I don't even know what I'm looking at here. There are no dates, no quantities."

"It was a negligible amount," he said. "The real excavation hasn't even started yet."

"How are we supposed to monitor the quality and extraction volume if there's no record of what's been removed?"

"Look, Jim, I'm not a high ranking official in a regulatory agency. I'm only the blockhead who gets this fancy future drug out the *goddamned* ground." Artie made a shovel out of his hand and stuck it in an invisible hole while he stared at me, then threw the invisible excavation over his shoulder. "You do you, and I'll do me. As the kids say."

I skirted Artie to grab the sludge-end of the coffee, glared and exhaled my dissatisfaction, rooted around in the extended mess for our ubiquitous can of coffee.

Discovered it behind a few discarded DFAC to-go boxes in various states of full and rotting.

Uncovered it. Empty.

I fished a new one out of the cabinet, unscrewed the top, popped the pressure tab, slipped a filter into the pot, and shook in a modest amount.

Artie rolled his eyes at me.

"Making some coffee-flavored water again?"

I ignored him and I screwed the lid on. It ran off the threads. I unscrewed it and tried again. Nope. Spun worthlessly in its tracks. I could feel Artie staring at me. This was how we lost the last coffee, though I have no idea where moisture came from. There wasn't any for miles. Until I did a bad job of closing the coffee, then it appeared.

I unscrewed the lid. Really stared at the jar. Lined things up.

Artie swooped in, plucked the lid and jar from my hands, opened the trailer door, and tossed both out into the desert.

"What the hell did you do that for?"

"Saved us all some good time and energy. We both know that coffee wasn't getting sealed for freshness. You're a coffee terrorist. No wonder you're so sympathetic to your terrorist friends."

Artie pulled a new jar out of the cupboard and put it in its rightful spot near the coffee maker.

"May as well use these once and throw 'em into the trash," he said. "MRI'll pay for it."

I rolled my eyes. MRI would pay for things but not people. Not *local* people, anyway.

"Rejoice and be glad, Jim. You're getting help today."

"What?"

"They emailed it in yesterday. One of your FDA cronies is on the hook now too. They're dropping him off today."

"Great. Nothing better than three men working nonstop together in two tiny trailers."

Inside I was relieved.

I SHIELDED my face from the dust storm of the chopper, awaiting our new colleague. No need to let the poor bastard suffer out there like I had when I first arrived. The sand blasted the few exposed body parts it could get—an earlobe, the tip of my nose, a bit of my ankle. I squinted at the new arrival, so far a dusty shadow, then a little bit clearer.

Salwar kameez, Pashtun style, plus one of those wooly Masood caps. Rahim and Artie were always trying to push one on me. It somehow had the opposite of the intended effect, made me even more out of place. This guy wore it well. My face heated when I recalled how I'd tried to cling to the chopper for dear life. Was he an Afghan? Not in his walk, he wasn't. Couldn't have been. He was supposed to be coming from the FDA. His gait was easy.

I squinted into the dust. Ravi. It was *Ravi* in there.

"No way!" I shouted.

Ravi waved and jogged up to me.

"Look at you," he yelled over the noise. "My very own Afghan welcoming party!"

"Can't believe they sent you to stink up my trailer!" I shouted. I clapped him on the back.

I teared up, and then I turned and wiped my eyes.

"Sand," I lied.

I was so relieved to see somebody I knew, I was crying like a sissy. If not for the searing heat, the helicopter sandstorm, I would have been able to take a good, deep breath for the first time in weeks. I was suffering this new brand of loneliness, though I'd been more interactive in the past week or two than in the whole rest of my previous life combined. It was a different kind of isolation, the isolation of being way in over my head. Way, way, way in over my head.

"WELL, THIS HAS BEEN FUN," Artie said. "I can't say it hasn't. But I have to do a run out to Site B, take some verification photos and scans to send back to home office."

"Okay, man." Ravi said. "It was nice to meetcha."

Rahim and I exchanged glances: mine full of panic, his full of acceptance. I'd come clean to Rahim late last week: I hadn't actually had a chance to talk to Artie about the inspections program yet.

Correction: I'd had plenty of chances. I just hadn't done it.

Artie grabbed his sunglasses off the top of a pile of crumpled invoices.

"Smell you all later," he said.

"I forgot my phone over at Site B," Rahim blurted out. He was a terrible liar. "I need to go anyway. I can do it."

This trailer reeked of guilt and garlic and body odor.

Artie shrugged. "Less work for me," he said. He threw his sunglasses back onto the invoices and stalked over to his desk, where he started an intensive phone-staring session.

I stifled my inhale and exhale of deep and terrified relief.

Ravi twitched an elbow at our lousy, burned up coffee pot. "Real bachelor pad in here," he said.

"Oh just you wait," I waved towards Artie's desk. "The smells that come from over there are unbelievable."

Artie twirled his hand from top-of-head to chin and bowed deeply. Ravi laughed. "Wanna show me the goods?"

"Yes. Let's walk Rahim out."

The three of us stepped out into the sunblast.

"You got everything under control over there, Rahim?"

"Yes, Mr. Jim. I do now," Rahim said. We exchanged a glance in which I acknowledged my cowardice, promised I would do the needful ASAP. Rahim nodded back his intimate knowledge that I was full of shit and wasn't rushing to do anything. He got into his ancient Corolla and rolled away, leaving an extended puff of dust in his wake.

"But he's okay, right?"

"Rahim? Sure."

"No, Artie."

"I think so," I said. I had no idea.

"They wouldn't put just anybody out here. On the Mineral X project. I mean, a lot's riding on this."

"Like what?"

At first, Ravi looked at me like I was kidding. He waited a long moment for me to divulge all my insider info. I saw a horror dawn on him when he realized I *actually* knew nothing. He took a deep breath. Then he leaned in.

"The day of the explosion at work."

"I *knew* it," I said. I didn't know it. I didn't even know what *it* was. I was trying to redeem myself by pretending I knew something.

"The day of the explosion at work, I injected every single one of those chubby little bastards with a serum composed of Mineral X."

"Did *you* blow up your own lab?"

"No," Ravi said. And I believed him. "Back to the rats."

"Okay. The rats."

Ravi pulled out his phone and flipped up a picture, to reveal four of the most svelte, dashing rats this world might have ever known.

"Jesus. They look like the Swedish version of rats."

Ravi withdrew his rat pic and narrowed his eyes. "Why'd you say Swedish?"

"No reason," I said. "I was just thinking of a creature that was thin and blond. If you put a blond wig on that one on the right it would look like the lady from ABBA."

The explanation seemed to satisfy him.

Diane's conspiracy theory: the *real* problem, the Swedes. The *Swedes*?

"You don't know the half of it. They don't age anymore. Some of them de-aged. They lost the weight. They lost their whole list of mental problems. Chromosome damage actually *reversed*. They gained in mental acuity, reflexes. Everything in them approved, all indicators, across the board. It's...it's incredible."

"Not just a weight loss drug."

"No. No, it's much more than that." Ravi said. "In the past five years, there's been a spike in hypermorbid obesity in the United States. Now, medically speaking, obesity isn't real. Neither is BMI. These are bullshit diagnoses invented by insurance companies based on, like, two studies of Danish people in the 1950s."

"Literally?"

"No. But you get what I'm saying. It's mostly a shame industry. Not science. You know."

I looked down at my stomach. "What do you mean, *you* know?"

Ravi ignored me. "In the United States, especially in the past ten years, we've seen a dramatic increase in this particular kind of weight gain, largely due to binge eating in such a quantity, and so repetitive over a compressed timeframe as to cause permanent metabolic dysfunction."

I thought about my pie eating at the DFAC. Surely that didn't count.

"This isn't normal weight gain from overeating," Ravi said.

It was a really good pie. What the hell was I supposed to do?

"It's disproportionate. In these cases, we're seeing appetite—that was typically controlled by forming memories, is now unchecked."

"By memories?"

"Yes. You can remember that you're full. So you stop eating. We discovered the hypermorbid obesity is being caused by a malfunction in *memory*—the subject suffers a perpetual amnesia about feeling full —total hypothalamus malfunction. Due to a lack of GIP in the body."

More acronyms. It was like being back at the FDA in here now that Ravi had arrived. I stared wordlessly at him until he relented with:

"Gastric inhibitory polypeptide. It's a hormone that stimulates insulin secretion."

I continued to stare blankly until Ravi said, "Don't worry about it. All you need to know is, there is a rare earth mineral. One rare earth mineral, in the whole world, and that mineral binds to GIP and acts like a super-receptor."

"Mineral X," I said.

"Mineral X," Ravi nodded. "It fixes everything, and a few more things besides."

"Have you seen it?"

"Not in its natural habitat."

I motioned for him to follow, and led Ravi out of the shade of the trailer, down the concrete steps, to its eerie pit in the earth.

"Heals osteoporosis, resolves metabolic malfunction to normalcy within months, cures pancreatic cancer and epilepsy, halts Alzheimer's, and resolves all forms of diabetes—"

"No shit?"

"No shit. And the only known deposits are located right here in Afghanistan."

"Are you sure?"

"I'm sure. This one's the largest. The CIA is sure. Every asshole who sends some troops to invade Afghanistan is sure. And they sent me here to be double and triple sure. Only thing I know is, everybody wants it. We gotta get this out of the ground. Quick."

I opened my mouth to run Diane's farfetched BPA-espionage theory by him. After everything he had said, it didn't seem so bizarre anymore.

"Hey ladies," Artie barked from the top step. I jumped. "Enjoying the view?"

I wondered if he'd heard us talking.

And I wondered what he knew about Mineral X.

19

WHY DID THE

"Why did the Russians invade Afghanistan?"

Ravi and his Socratic method, asking questions I didn't care about that he knew the answer to while I was burning under the Afghan sun at high noon.

Rahim was late in picking us up.

"It was about Communism. To spread Communism, right? They were Commies." I leaned over the railing. At least if I fell into the mine it would be cooler. And I wouldn't have to face whatever was going on over at Site B.

"Right, and then why did the US invade Afghanistan? To spread freedom?"

"Uh, yeah, to bring Democracy. We brought Democracy. They're a Democracy now." I gestured at the landscape around me to indicate all the freedom and democracy we were witnessing on a daily basis.

Ravi looked at me like I was an idiot. I felt like an idiot. We both looked at the big hole in the ground.

"You think it was this," I finally said. "Mineral X."

"No country has ever invaded another country for non-financial reasons, Jim."

Ravi kicked a pebble off the concrete steps and into the pit. We listened for it but couldn't hear it hit bottom. "Think for a second about how America used to be. In 1945, we beat the Nazis. We had the greatest fighting force in the world. We were conquerors. Liberators. We were lean and mean and we kicked *ass*."

"I mean, I don't think it was that easy."

"When's the last time you saw the United States kick any ass, Jim? We haven't won a war since. Americans are so fat these days we can barely walk down the street."

"Oh, come on Ravi." I self-consciously sucked in my own gut. "It's not all that bad. Look at us. We're still mobile."

"The Nazis used to sneak spies into America. The Russians did too. When the Cold War started, I think they snuck something else in."

Ravi was turning out to be a real *Diane*. Nothing but conspiracy theories from morning to night. Ever since he arrived.

I relented. "Are you going to tell me what?"

"Endocrine disrupters."

"BPA?"

"How'd you know?"

"Diane—"

"*DEA* Diane?"

"Yeah. DEA Diane. You know her?"

"I know *of* her. Never met. She still working on the poppy fields?"

"I don't know," I said. I realized I didn't know what Diane worked on. It had never come up. "But I do know this: the Russians don't make me eat pecan pie every night. I think we'd better get inside. Rahim's late. And your conspiracy theories are giving me chest pains." My chest *did* hurt, or maybe that was my stomach. I was sweating out everything I had, too. We were probably both heat-stroking. Hard.

Maybe just me. Ravi looked fine. I turned to head inside and after a moment I heard Ravi follow.

"Say what you want, Jim, but there's a lot of geopolitical and financial power in rendering the richest country on the earth much fatter and dumber, and then selling the cure for it back to them."

I wanted to argue, but I couldn't really come up with anything, it was so hot, and bright, and I was too out of breath, so I said nothing. We trudged in silence after that.

It was an interesting theory, but I had bigger problems.

Site B secret inspections training program that your volatile colleague opposed, problems.

———————————

TWO HOURS AND ONE LONG, hot, shock-absorption-free Toyota Corolla ride later, Ravi, Rahim, and I stood in a tent that could have housed a three-ring circus.

And it *was* a kind of three-ring circus in there: a mined mineral, bio-medical, illicit inspections, three-ring circus.

That I had approved.

"Eight inspectors, Rahim. That's how many I thought we were agreeing to."

"Eight volunteers aren't nearly enough, Mr. Jim," Rahim said. He looked embarrassed, ashamed. It had to be a defense tactic. It just had to be.

"Artie's gonna kill you," Ravi said. He kicked a miscellaneous burlap sack, one of dozens that lined one side of the tent.

"Oh, yeah, you think?" I snapped back.

The tiniest little volunteer snaked his way through no fewer than eighty workstations and then fell over pushing a wheelbarrow full of dirt into the middle of the tent. Glittery dirt scattered across the floor. He picked himself up quickly and started scooping the dirt back into the wheelbarrow with both hands.

I looked away, but there wasn't a thing in there I could rest my eyes on without becoming enraged.

"Are you employing children, Rahim?"

"He's eighteen," Rahim said.

"Bullshit," Ravi said. But I didn't think he had much skin in this game.

"We weren't expecting you today," Rahim said.

"But you picked us up," Ravi pointed out. "And brought us here."

Rahim tugged on his beard. That was indisputable.

"I don't know how to explain this," I said. "I don't know how to pay for this, and I don't know how to explain this."

There had been an incessant drilling since we'd arrived. Not the mining—no, that hadn't even begun yet, at Site A *or* Site B. The drilling noise was just an army of young adults *or* teenagers *or* underage pre-teens, I couldn't tell, assembling what appeared to be *infinity* number of workstations on the fringes of the most massive tent.

"It's Thursday," Rahim said. "We were, ah, about to conclude work for the day."

"Rahim, we've got to put a stop to this."

"Please," he said. "It would be a great honor if you both would join us at my home for lunch."

A big gust of wind caught the closest tent flap and yanked its stake right out of the ground. I was gonna lose my mind.

"You know, every time you want something it's this damn charm offensive and I'm sick of—"

"I *am* super hungry," Ravi said.

"For fuck's sake," I said.

Rahim appealed to me with the menu. "My wife is making Kabuli Pulao."

A loud metallic crash and a scream of pain came from the work-station assembly area.

"They'll be fine," he said. "Don't worry."

"Kabuli Pulao," Ravi said. "Sounds great."

"Don't blame yourself," the doctor said. In some ways I blamed myself, but in other ways I took no responsibility at all. It was the medical device manufacturer's fault. It was the doctor's fault. It was the hospital's fault. It was the government's fault. I am the government, I know, but I didn't think that phrase while thinking about myself, walking to the building every day where the device was supposed to be regulated, where patients were supposed to be kept safe by a foolproof team of genius who knew everything about everything: food and drugs and mesh that got shoved into women's goddamned vaginas.

Yeah, right.

I allowed myself to think about the whole situation so ephemerally that it didn't even exist in reality. I never really saw her, Elise, saw my children, in that bathtub. In that bathroom. Saw what had happened. I didn't register any of it at all. Their deaths. My life. I didn't see these facts laid out before me.

So I didn't grieve. And I hid, I hid from work, I hid from my family, I hid from Elise's family, I hid from our mutual friends. Until I didn't exist at all. And then somebody saw me. And sent me to Afghanistan. And now, all of a sudden, I'm alive again and I notice that I'm alive. And I notice that Elise isn't here, and the kids aren't here.

"More pulao?"

"Yes, please," I said.

Rahim's wife scooped another heaping plate together and handed it to me, as if I hadn't already eaten one, not to mention the appetizer course and five other dishes on the table.

They were trying to kill me with food.

"I ought to use the bathroom," I said. I felt a little bit dizzy for no real reason. My heart was working overtime, felt like, once my stomach was full. I worked hard to get up off the ground. People in Afghanistan had to be spry until the day they died. There was no choice, there was no furniture.

I paused my hand washing and stared at myself in the mirror, hard.

Those little miracles are gone forever. How can I still be living without them. I walk and I talk, I do a fuckup job at eating another woman's pussy. And where is my first family? What did I allow? How could I have stopped it? A thousand ways, I'm sure. When the golf ball hits a blade of grass, the grass thinks wow, I'm one in a million. But it could have been any blade of grass.

Who am I to think I'm a special blade of grass?

Everybody was done eating by the time I re-joined the meal.

"Feeling alright?" Ravi asked. He was picking his teeth with the customary after-dinner toothpick.

"Yeah," I said. "Long day."

"The children want to take us on a walk," Ravi said. "Up for it?"

They were flanking him on either side and had obviously been waiting for me, their little faces expectant.

"Sure," I said. "Why not?"

We headed out into the backyard, out the gate, and down the dirt alley. The sun was setting and the first few stars were already visible. Rahim's little girl trailed her fingers along a mud-spackled retaining wall and snuck a peek back at me, every here and there.

"I miss my kids," Ravi said.

"Oh, do you have children?" Rahim asked.

"Two. Just about these ages, too."

"Children are a gift," Rahim said. "How about you, Mr. Jim? Do you have a family?"

"They died unexpectedly," I said.

His eyes widened. It was rare for Westerners to experience a similar level of loss to those in non-Western countries. That's what I imagined he was thinking. I always pretended I could read minds. I'd done that to Elise a lot too. I don't know why.

"All of them?"

"Yes," I said. "My wife and two kids."

Something in Rahim's face told me he knew not to ask how they died.

"How did they die?" He asked.

Wrong again. Faking psychic ability while not psychic.

"They drowned," I said. Technically true, except for Elise. I didn't owe anybody the truth.

"That must have been awful," Rahim said. "I'm so sorry." And a tear escaped his eye. This was the second time I'd seen this in Afghanistan, and it shocked me. I had never seen a human moved to tears about the plight of another human, not on a screen or through manipulated means.

The first time it was second-hand info. Diane had told me that the local security lady at work was crying so much she was totally distracted, and anybody could have gotten through. What was the issue? I'd asked. Another woman on the team had suffered some domestic violence. Another woman, or her?

Another woman, Diane confirmed. Yeah, I know, crazy. Empathy. Who knew it was possible? Not us, I'd said. Not us.

Rahim's overt feeling reminded me I'd had a feeling about it once, too.

My whole body went cold and my hands went cold and my stomach clenched until I screamed and coughed and the water over-spilling onto the floor and their bodies, their little crumpled bodies and clothes my vomit out in the hall and banging my head on the floor until I bled and Elise in there on the floor and me on the floor

and hate

filling my head

and choking

"It's okay," I said. But it wasn't. "I mean, thank you."

Rahim's son and daughter led Ravi, Rahim, and me down a side path through a field. The dusty haze down by our feet when we walked gave way to a green carpet full of wildflowers. Rahim's daughter picked something off the ground and gave it to her dad, then made him stop, and crouch down, so she could whisper to him.

"She wants you to see this leaf is shaped like a heart," Rahim said. He handed it to me. It was so small and green. And it was shaped like a heart.

Something broke loose inside my chest then, a low level of pain and pressure I hadn't known I still carried.

I turned my face away and I wiped a tear off the covered side. Rahim might have noticed what was happening and took the kids up ahead so I would have a moment. Ravi trailed them. I saw Rahim explaining something to both of them, gesturing and looking back at me.

What was he saying? He had a family once, but they died. It must have been a simple and straightforward explanation, because the kids were nodding. The boy walked up ahead to grab a rock and throw it into the *kariz*, the little ditch that served as graywater transport here. The girl looked back at me.

Was I getting better or worse? Maybe I was just acknowledging for the first time since they died that I had a family once. A wife and two kids. Since their deaths they were flashes of memory here and there, concepts in my mind. How did you know what was real? They weren't there to tell you who they had been after all. However you remembered them, that's what they were.

I caught up to the group.

"Tell her I said thank you," I said. I twirled the heart-shaped leaf. I thought it would make her happy, and it seemed to. "I'll figure things out with Artie," I said to Rahim.

20

WE'VE GOT COMPANY

"We've got company tomorrow," Artie announced. Then he belched into the open air between us. Coffee and something rancid. Maybe last night's Big Mac at Bagram.

"Oh?" I said.

"Delegation. A few Chinese businessmen, a Senator or twelve. Some Swedes, maybe. We'll get the list from the Consulate tomorrow."

The Chinese, the Senate, and Swedes?

"Swedes?"

Artie shrugged. "That's what the cable said."

"Do we have to do something?"

"Nah, they'll send security to do a sweep and a scout the day before. And they'll pair 'em with a tank or two."

"Big production."

"Always is. Can't do anything small here. Tee-Eye-Ay." TIA. This is Afghanistan.

"Alright," I said. "Should I attend?" I peered into the depths of the coffee pot. Artie had reheated yesterday's and turned it into a meaty sludge already.

"I'll tell you one thing." Artie stood up.

He knows.

My heart thumped so hard it seemed to me he could hear it. I flushed. My damn face always betrayed me.

Artie stopped swiping on his phone and sat back down.

I sighed. It came out trembling, my breath. "Listen, Artie."

He seemed to change his mind about something on the phone, and he set it on his desk. Face down.

"You think I don't know?" He was next to me in a flash. I thought he was going to hit me, and I flinched.

Instead, he grabbed the canister of coffee and shook nearly the whole damn thing into a new filter in the top of the maker.

"Artie, I agreed to a small pilot test. That's all."

"I don't care what you agreed to, you little weasel. You compromised the security of our whole project, exposed us to a bunch of terrorists—"

"They're not terrorists, Artie. They're college kids who want a fair opportunity."

"Well, you should have thought about that before you engaged them in this illegal activity, because they're gonna be rounded up like they're terrorists. Detained like they're terrorists. Most likely *jailed* like they're terrorists. That's the punishment for illegal mining."

"Mining? Hell, they took a wheelbarrow of dirt out of the ground and you're treating them like—"

"And I ought to have you arrested too. How'd you like that, Jimbo? You wanna spend a year or twelve in Pul-e-Charkhi?"

"They're innocent, Artie. They haven't done anything wrong."

"The authorities will be the judge of that. And they've already razed Site B."

"No."

"Yes. I'm not asking you, *princess*. I'm telling you." Artie slammed the coffee pot into place. It shattered into three pieces, the handle still in his hand. With the color drained out of his face, I could see every single crag and crevice much clearer, somehow. He was a much older man than I'd noticed, all these days, who'd covered it in snark and a spry way of moving himself about.

"Artie, are you—"

"Now look what you made me do," he snapped. I was shaking. I couldn't handle confrontation to save my life. "Just go do a quick sweep of the first fifty feet of Site A. Kick the debris off the path. You know, so one of the Senators doesn't trip in his fancy shoes and break a hip." He threw the handle in the trash. "I'll clean this mess up."

"Alright," I said. "No problem." But he left the shards of glass where they lay, went back to his desk, picked up his phone, and started swiping again.

I saw myself out.

I KICKED a red rock out of the way.

Fuck Artie, I mumbled, like I was a teenager and he was my dad. I was so scared of him. Why?

Down and down. I adjusted my headlamp to do all the work the strings of LEDs couldn't do. Whoever had started this excavation of Mineral X, they'd gotten pretty far in. It was deeper and darker than LEDs had a chance of illuminating.

I peered over the edge of the path, down a few levels to the last layer visible.

There was a deep crater down there, a horizontal hole single-mindedly dug down like a big dog had pawed up the earth for a bone. Revealed the series of red streaks I'd come to know as Mineral X. I squinted at it. Noticed a gleam.

Like nothing I'd ever seen before.

Next to the red.

A cool blue. A cool, shimmering, miraculous blue. It reminded me of the color of Ally's eyes when she was first born, or the sky after a heavy rain.

In my next breath, I was down there. At it. Next to it. Like I woke up there. No memory of getting there. Far away. Blink. Up close.

I neared it. If I reached out and touched it, what would it feel like?

I *was* reaching out and touching it.

Out of reach of the last LED light, lit by headlamp alone.

It grazed my fingertips, a flash. Light that came from the inside of my eyes. Twisting inside my skull. I was there and I was me and then I'd been snapped into a group chat happening in my own brain, crowding out my own thoughts. I heard Artie, I heard Rahim, I heard the chatter of a few voices that sounded familiar but whose language I didn't understand.

Then I *did* understand, knew the concepts behind the words, the visuals and the feelings, I reached out and I touched that stone, was I touching it? When did—

And I heard Artie's voice above all others:

"Blow him the fuck up."

I was speaking it and I was hearing it, I was Artie and I was the mind of an Afghan youth, scared, hiding the future explosion in a cooking oil can, running it into Site A, sitting a hill away, holding my real Nokia and my fake one, waiting for the order. From Artie.

I was watching the site cameras from my desk, waiting for me to descend, giving the order into my phone.

To kill me.

THE WALL of dirt on my right crumbled, muffled by my new mental reach but immediate, the ringing in my ears, the flash of the explosion, the rock raining. I was under a pillar, a pillar that Mineral X and whatever was next to it had caught, rubble all around me.

All around. Cradling me. But not crushing me.

I wriggled my arms and legs.

I panted and choked. My headlamp was gone. Coughed big wheezing gasps that set my throat on fire.

Then I tried again to move my arms and legs. All free, untrapped. I scooted myself out, beyond the jagged edge of the fallen pillar. Opened and closed my hands. Sneezed the raw dust out of the back of my throat.

The voices in my head were gone. The gleam next to Mineral X wasn't visible anymore. It was covered in debris.

I picked myself up from the ground, dusted myself off, and pawed my way back to the trailer in the darkness.

I'd not been blown the fuck up after all.

I REACHED for the handle to the trailer. A little dust dervish was getting going behind me. Dirt clung to my sweat, lined the inside of my gums, all over from head to toe. Before I could open the door, it opened for me.

Artie looked surprised.

"Hi," I said.

"Well well well," Artie said. "What happened here?"

You know damn well what happened here, I didn't say.

I couldn't read the expression on his face, if he respected me because I didn't die right on time. Like I was a formidable prey. Probably not.

"I guess the sweep is done."

"Yeah," I said. "You got that right." I pooched out my lower lip to exhale a stream of dirt out of my hair, avalanche it onto the trailer floor. "All clear down there now. Ready for visiting dignitaries." I brushed past him to hit the lone shower in the back.

21

YOU TRIED TO

"Y ou tried to kill me, you miserable piece of shit," I said.
     I pointed into the mirror above the compost toilet in my trailer closet that pretended it was a bathroom. Cost a billion dollars, I was sure of it. Was MRI billing the FDA for this crap? Push-button water faucet eked out a disappointing rust-colored stream every fourth or fifth try. No shower.

This was my fifteenth or sixteenth round since I'd anxiety-roused myself at 3 am. I still didn't look menacing. What was to prevent Artie from killing me right there, in person?

Rahim would be around. Hopefully. And then there was Ravi, but he was in and out, flying around from this base to that, doing his samples, running his tests, chattering away exclusively in acronyms by now and mostly to himself, mad scientist gone madder.

I pushed the water button again to blast the shave cream off my disposable razor. Wasn't enough pressure to budge it one bit.

Tough to say if Artie cared much about *that*: witnesses. Basically, Artie could do whatever the hell he wanted. Unfettered by rule of law. Unprosecuted. Or MRI would show up with a team of lawyers and he'd stride away from my corpse scot-free.

What would I gain from confronting him?

I couldn't think of anything. But how could I not confront him? The work relationship hadn't been great before, but now it'd come to a murder attempt.

Also: what the hell happened to me down there? Was I having a psychotic break?

Maybe the explosion was an accident, all the voices, a hallucination: a stress memory. People said things like that all the time to me after Elise. Blamed her brain and not her. Said stress did it. But how much can you blame everything on stress? Is Artie just trying to kill me because he's stressed? Is that admissible in court these days?

I had to, Your Honor. I was *stressed*.

Oh, okay. Case dismissed. Gavel slam.

If Elise had lived, after the children *didn't*, she would have been prosecuted. The State of Maryland would have prosecuted the *shit* out of her. Or the county, or whatever. I was sure of that. People hated mothers for messing up on the job. Even when it wasn't their fault.

I buttoned up my shirt, pulled on my workboots, and clomped out across our makeshift dirt and dust avenue to do the deed: more confrontation. Since it had worked so well the last time.

At least I'd made it through the night. I could have called a chopper to get me the hell out of there, to sleep back at my CHU like I used to, but after I'd rinsed off the explosion dust my brain was reeling so hard with the shock I couldn't do much of anything. I'd decided Artie wouldn't try to kill me a second time in one day, not the wisest decision I've ever made, and I'd passed out on the cot in my FDA trailer.

And it seemed like he hadn't. Tried. To kill me. Again, last night.

I took a deep breath, and I stepped in to face my would-be murderer.

"Morning," Artie called from his desk. He didn't even look up.

Or the try was very subtle.

"Morning," I said.

Say it, just say it. Why could I never produce the words I wanted to, when I wanted to? This was ridiculous. My coworker tried to kill me, and I was hoping to sweep that under the rug?

"Artie—" I started.

"There's a message for you," Artie said. He slapped his phone down, sprang up from his desk, dumped about a pound of coffee into a filter and plopped it into the coffeemaker. He pointed at the table with the pot.

A new, unbroken pot. He sure got that fast. Must have had it choppered in?

I picked up the note and read it.

"What the hell is this?"

"Don't ask me," he said. "I guess Uncle Sam's got another job for you."

"Is this a prank?" I asked.

"Doesn't look like it," he said. "Looks like a cable. From the State Department. To you."

"To me?"

"Sending you to South Africa."

"South Africa."

"Today," Artie said.

"What the hell?" I said. I slammed the note down on the filthy table.

Artie shrugged. "I guess skilled bureaucrats are in short supply," he said. "Anyway, try to look more in control and less shocked."

"Why?"

"Because the delegation will be here in fifteen."

"CARTEL TIME," Rahim said, sing-song, rocking back and forth on his heels.

He and I stood in the shade of the MRI trailer, facing the mine, waiting for our guests. Every time I called it a mine, Artie told me not to. He said it had been *amateur hour* up to that point and now that he and MRI were involved, I'd soon see what a real mine looked like.

Except I wouldn't.

Because I was going to be forcibly sent to South Africa in a few hours.

Wait, what did Rahim say?

"What?"

"I said, cartel time." Rahim fidgeted with a small loop of beads he usually kept in his pocket, flicking them back and forth.

"What do you mean, *cartel* time?"

"It's the cartel. I do not understand, Mr. Jim. What do you mean, what do I mean?"

"Rahim." I seized his shoulders with both hands. He didn't flinch. Man-on-man touching wasn't as much of a punishment in Afghanistan as it was in the United States. I was suffering more than he was. I let go. "Are you saying *this* is *the* cartel?"

"Yes. Did you *not* know this is the cartel?"

"*I* thought the cartel was a bunch of Afghan warlords. Afghan. Warlords. *Afghans*. Who controlled the poppy fields. Terrorized you. Threw a brick through your window now and then."

"Oh, no, Mr. Jim. The cartel is a group of Senators. From USA."

Rahim and I watched a seemingly endless convoy of Suburbans stream off Jalalabad Road and invade our tiny worksite, creating a mushroom cloud of dust. We choked and covered our mouths and choked some more.

"Why didn't you tell me that?" I choked.

"I thought you knew." Rahim shrugged, choking. "I thought they were your bosses. Are you not American?"

"Yes, but—"

Artie emerged from the trailer, cutting our vital exchange of choked-out info short, before I even got to the part where Artie had tried to kill me, and knew everything there was to know about Site B, and was planning to retaliate in the most poisonous way possible, and, oh, by the way, I was getting shipped to South Africa for reasons unknown.

He extended his left arm far out in front of him and pulled back on the fingers with his right hand, then switched arms and hands and repeated.

"Gentlemen, get ready to shake some hands," he said to me and Rahim. The lead Suburban opened its doors. Artie adjusted his own collar, ran his fingers through his hair, grinned at me, smirked a hole right through my head until I turned away and plastered a smile on my own face.

Cleared his throat. Gently. Like he was gonna sing an opera.

———————

SENATOR TOM FLETCH Senior was a man who, if he smiled, when he smiled, if he did that, and all his teeth were filed into sharp points, and then after he smiled, he shook your hand, and after he shook your hand, he put your hand into his mouth and bit the whole thing off, I would have said, later on, makes sense.

Makes a lot of sense.

Not a surprise at all.

He didn't smile, though.

His massive paw dwarfed my soft and clammy. Pumped me up and down. He was wearing a full suit and not sweating. I was coated, and dripping in the spots I'd shaved that morning, sweat glands working overtime to get through a shave cream residue that hadn't quite rinsed off.

"Call me Tom," he said.

"Fletch Industries," I heard, not from him though. It was a murmur in his entourage. I wondered what the relation was, if any.

Sixteen more handshakes to go.

I was shaking Pauly's hands on autopilot, one and then the other before I knew it, before I knew I knew them.

"Well hello there, man of the hour. I've been hearing about you lately," Polly said without tone or voice inflection or any hint of what she'd been hearing.

Was it about Site B?

"Heard you're on your way to South Africa," Paul chimed in.

"About that—" I said. "—I need—"

"Let's talk later," Polly shut me down and continued on the handshake tour.

"Lanna. Bergström." The most beautiful neck that had ever graced this earth. "Swedish delegate."

The Swedes. Diane's 'real' threat. I saw the threat now. This woman was too goddamned good looking. Made me feel sick. I scanned down the line for Diane. Was this a DEA party, too? Maybe, but no Diane.

"Jim," I apologized to Lanna Bergström for my own appearance with my eyes, and kept moving. I had no business associating with a neck like that.

I made it through the whole lot, five more Senators besides, and a few aides, the ambassador and some titles I forgot immediately, a member of the press who didn't identify his newspaper or television station or tweeting handle or blog or whatever the hell press meant these days.

None of the men with guns around us shook hands or were introduced. I guessed that wasn't the function of the security detail, necessarily, to learn the names and faces of people while they were building evidence on whether or not to gun them or somebody else in the area down.

Nobody shook hands with Rahim, who was edged further behind me and Artie with each case of negligence to shake hands by every single attendee.

"Shall we?" Senator Fletch boomed. And then he said, "Come on, boy." At first, I thought he was talking to Rahim. But then the crowd parted, and revealed a kid with his face shoved in an iPad.

The guy brought his *kid* on a field trip to Afghanistan.

Off we went.

He walked up front like he owned the mining site and all of us on it, leading us to the concrete steps rather than the other way around.

Artie motioned for me to follow, and dragged me, sweating and puffing, up to trail the overly speedy heels of Senator Fletch and his son.

"Senator," Artie said. Sheen in his eye.

Whatever you're going to say, you son of a bitch, *don't*.

"I've got a hunch," he said.

"Well, Artie. What's your hunch?"

Artie. Were they old friends or did they just meet?

"More than a hunch, actually. Some intel. For you. We've got another site, not as far along as this one. But my intel says that it's compromised."

"Compromised. How?"

"By terrorists," Artie said.

I couldn't breathe or see anything except Senator Fletch's heels, tamping down the dust in front of my own feet.

"Terrorists," Fletch agreed. We made it to the concrete steps. Senator Fletch stopped in his tracks and gripped the railing with both hands to await his entourage, chirping and trailing behind him from mine to Suburban row.

"Yes, sir. Terrorists. I'm not saying we can't use the site eventually. But it'll be best for you to call in a carpet bomb. Poppy activity, you know. DEA can handle the paperwork. Part of the larger eradication program. Funds ISIS. Easy to Raptor it. It's all been Alcis-verified, obviously. And we'll Bagger it later on in the year, anyway."

"Sure," Fletch said. "Happy to."

"How's tomorrow?" Artie winked at me.

"Will do," Fletch said.

I looked around for Rahim in a panic, my heart fluttering around in my chest. He wasn't anywhere that I could see.

"Are you okay, buddy?" Artie asked.

"Sure," I said. "Why?"

"Your color looks a little off," Artie said. "You're usually so pale you're borderline transparent, or heart attack red."

I flushed embarrassment and panicked at the same time. I could push him over. The Senator. I could barrel my shoulder right into him and we'd both go over the railing, fall a story or two down. Maybe live, maybe die, maybe break our backs, both of us, live the rest of our lives as quadripeligics, him in his fancy life, me in prison for attempted murder.

"Senator," Lanna Bergström said. "I don't understand your plan for getting it into every American on the eastern seaboard. Will it be through vaccination?"

"Lanna, my dear. People will wear it."

"Willingly?" She arched one beautifully thin and sculpted eyebrow.

"Watch this," he said. He seized the iPad from his son's hands and hurled it over the side of the mine.

The boy was much younger than I'd noticed at first, couldn't have been much older than seven, maybe eight years of age, tops. His expression moved from shock and terror into rage and withdrawal. Tears rolled down his cheeks.

"*NO*," he shouted, and climbed onto the railing, and I thought he was going to hurl *himself* over the side. I took a step forward to stop him.

Senator Tom Fletch Senior (R-NJ) closed his meaty palm over the boy's slender arm, leaned down, and said something that drained all the color out of his tiny, fine-boned face. He climbed down and stood there so utterly broken, I may as well have been looking at myself.

"I have to go pack," I said. "Excuse me, I have to go pack."

Lanna Bergström, Senator Fletch Senior, Senator Fletch Junior, and anybody else within earshot ignored me. Nobody was listening except Artie, and he said, "Don't let the door hit you in the ass on the way out, son."

22

IS EVERYBODY CRACKING

"**I**s everybody cracking up?" I offered the note for Ravi to read, paced back and forth another five times in my trailer. Ravi read it and shrugged.

"I don't know, man. They say you gotta go to South Africa, I don't know what choice you have. Once they start sending you places, they keep it up."

"Listen, they're going to carpet bomb Site B."

"Who is?"

"Those Senators. The cartel."

"Calm down," Ravi said. "You're not making a whole lot of sense right now."

"Artie just asked Senator Fletch to *Raptor* site B! Whatever the hell that means."

"Okay, well, a carpet bombing and the Raptor are two very different—"

"Yeah, right, I'm not a bombing-the-*shit*-out-of-things expert, okay? You have to tell Rahim, so he can get everybody to clear out of there. Now I can't find him, and they're shipping me—"

The loudening *thwacka thwacka thwacka* made me want to throw up. When I was a kid, I thought helicopters were so cool. Now I didn't ever want to see a helicopter again in my life. Ravi and I went outside. The Suburban parade was parked in its original places, no sign of its constituency, still haunting the mine.

The chopper touched down. A white guy dressed like an Afghan jumped out. His Ray Bans and folio betrayed him, besides his lily-white skin. He must have something to prove. Were westerners in foreign countries always this incorrigible? Or was it because we were in a country we'd invaded?

"Jim Schreiber?"

"Sure," I said. "Schneider," I shouted.

"Congrats. You won the ticket out. Pretoria."

"What for?"

"Official business."

"Official FDA business? In Pretoria?"

"Yep."

"Okay, so—"

"You're going straight to the airport. They packed you a bag for the duration of your detail."

"Is this a one-way ticket?"

"I don't have any further instructions for you. Whoever meets you at the airport ought to have more info."

"Did the FDA give you that outfit?"

Americans here didn't appreciate jokes. He thrust a piece of paper at me. Then he stalked inside Artie's trailer. What was he, my replacement? I didn't even have a chance to process this with Ravi. I looked back at him.

"Find Rahim and tell him," I shouted. He gave me the thumbs up. Nothing was a thumbs up right now.

I climbed on to the helicopter and unfolded my only clue.

LOCATION: Pretoria, South Africa
Length of stay: 7 days, to be extended upon request

TDY content: Aid in the extradition of Kwa Lele Odoki

I NEARLY PISSED MYSELF. FDA's ten most wanted, number three, eyes that burned a hole through you. Through me. I couldn't remember last year, last week, what I ate for breakfast this morning, but I could remember her picture in that PowerPoint, a million years ago. I flipped through the pages of the file, recalling all the terrifying details about her that a beefy man had announced to me in an obscure and irrelevant training.

Born 1980.

Uganda.

Leader of the female militia The Women's Liberation Army, created in part by siphoning off development funds and arranging false erectile dysfunction pharmaceutical sales.

Arrested.

Evaded extradition in Zambia.

Escaped.

Now detained in Pretoria and awaiting intervention by US officials to proceed.

ME?

I'm the US officials?

There was no good reason to expect me to interact with a terrifying criminal mastermind after I'd carefully manufactured a whole lifetime in a cubicle, hiding from people.

"Are you okay?" The co-pilot asked me.

"No," I said. "I don't think so."

"Are you gonna throw up?" He asked.

"Maybe," I said.

He tapped the pilot, made a vomiting gesture, thumb towards me. They both laughed. The pilot handed him a small paper bag, and he turned it over to me. I unfolded it and stared inside at nothing. At least here in Afghanistan there was a protocol for handling how not-okay I was. That was different from home.

But I wasn't going home anyway.

I was going to South Africa, while a bunch of Afghan children got carpet bombed in my wake.

We took off.

23

MY GUESTHOUSE IN

My guesthouse in Pretoria was a plush oasis teeming with government workers and unlikely foliage.

I was in shock.

A State Department official came by and briefed me moments after I arrived.

I was *still* in shock.

He said little more than the stupid piece of paper that had ordered me into this luxury leaf maze.

I listened to him, or I didn't, while in shock, calling Ravi in Afghanistan and listening to *that* go right to voicemail.

The next day, another one came around.

We sat on the edge of deck chairs near the pool, me looking ridiculous in my board shorts, him looking ridiculous in his overblown suit. A round little bird bobbed near my feet. I hated it for no reason. Where was my desert, my helicopters, my blinding sun? I wasn't cut out for this jet-setting, climate-changing lifestyle.

"Her name is Kwa Lele Odoki. She was born in 1980. In Uganda, according to her birth certificate. But she received that in a refugee camp, so it's unreliable."

"Okay," I said.

"She created a militia, it's called The Women's Liberation Army and about a dozen other names." He mopped his forehead. I was a sweaty mess too, I couldn't handle humidity anymore. "It's an all-female militia."

"Interesting. Doesn't seem FDA-relevant."

"She funded it by siphoning off development funds. That's why we're involved down at State. Could be some inside fraud. OIG is taking a look at it, too."

"Ok. Still not really part of our schtick. Food. Drugs."

"Oh, it's drugs. It's definitely drugs. The whole militia is financed by false erectile dysfunction pharmaceutical sales to the US."

I choked on my rooibos tea a little. I'd forgotten that part. What a criminal background. I looked up from my crotch at the same time he did and we both looked away: I picked the little bird again. Hopping obnoxiously.

What the hell are you doing here, bird?

"What's the army do?"

"Oh, you know. The usual terrorist shit."

What was the usual terrorist shit?

"Right," I said.

"She was arrested a year ago. She evaded extradition in Zambia and escaped. Killed someone in the process. Now ENACT nabbed her again. They set her up, plucked her right off the street. South African government is waiting for intervention by US officials to proceed."

"If she's got so much fake pill money, why didn't she just get a lawyer?"

"Whose side are you on?" He laughed the easy laugh of a man who would not be encountering a hardened international criminal that day. "Look, we need enough of an interview to clear the extradition process. It won't take much. We've got a script. Now we need you to read it."

"To her?"

"To her."

My mouth dried up.

"Over the phone?"

"In person."

"In person," I echoed. "Of course."

My voice was so far away from me.

"Are you okay?"

"People ask me that a lot," I said.

"You don't look okay," he said.

"Stomach thing," I said. And it felt true, just then. My stomach didn't feel great.

"Are you ready?"

"Now?"

"They're holding her downtown. In jail. So, yes. Now."

24

A MASSIVE STATUE

A massive statue of Nelson Mandela greeted me outside the jail. Wasn't he a political prisoner? He wouldn't have approved of this statue placement.

I was sweating all over my body. I wasn't fit to interview a militia leader, that was for sure. My hands shook. The folio that contained their dumb interview slipped out of my sweaty hands, and hit the ground open. A gust of wind picked up the interview, and I chased it all the way across the parking lot until I finally managed to plant my foot in its center.

It was inexplicable to me that this wasn't something outsourced to *any* South African police officer, investigator, or other more suitable individual who would be accustomed to dealing with hardened criminals. No. They had to get the dumbest, wimpiest guy at the FDA to do it. Who had previously been even more inexplicably posted to Afghanistan.

Pep talk. Okay, your life is pretty much over anyway, and you just killed a bunch of kids, so if this woman kills you and eats you, it doesn't even matter.

No wonder Elise killed herself. It was to get away from this kind of chit-chat.

The warden was cheerful. Beautifully dressed. Would have been a great candidate for conducting this interview with a mass murderer.

"Mr. Schneider." He gripped my hand. "Thank you so much for coming down. Rght this way."

I followed him down the hallway. It didn't look that bad. I'd expected something out of a movie, I suppose.

"Miss Odoki is a real handful," the warden said. "We will be relieved to turn her over to your government's care."

"You're not turning her over to my care."

"No, of course not," he agreed.

It was bare bones, and there weren't any bugs. I don't know why I expected the rest of the world to look like an Indiana Jones movie set, full of snakes and creepie crawlies.

He rubbed his hands together. I didn't understand why he looked so happy, what was in it for him. Did you get a bonus from the USG for calling in an extradition? I doubted it. Nobody liked a rat. Maybe Viagra was going to comp him for protecting the sanctity of their patent.

Rats. Fat rats. Dead, carpet-bombed kids in Afghanistan because of fat rats in America.

"Thank you. Listen, will there be, uh, protection?"

A woman in jail because she sold fake dick drugs.

"For her or for you?" He chuckled.

"For me. Obviously. She'll be fine, I'm sure."

"Certainly!" He scratched his nose with the key. "There is an outer and inner door. Just outside the inner door, we will have posted an armed guard. If you need anything, shout!"

"You think I'll survive between the time I shout and the time that guard gets in there?"

The sound of the jail cell door slamming open made me jump. I was all riled up. This couldn't be going any worse.

I gulped.

"Kwa Lele Odoki?"

"Yes."

She sat at the table. It was bolted down, so she couldn't vivisect me with it. She was smaller in person than I'd imagined her, because I'd been spending all my days and nights imagining a giant, brandishing her AK-47s and shoving them into the clammy, sniveling orifices of any unwitting FDA employee who tried to interview her.

Her orange jumpsuit billowed about her, and her wrists looked too small for the handcuffs, as if she could slip right out of them.

Maybe she could.

What was all this about? That's what I really wanted to ask her.

Instead, I sat down in the metal chair opposite her. Set down my folio, cleared my throat. I'm a big government official from America. I tried to puff up my caved, underdeveloped chest.

I took the crumpled script with my footprint in the middle of it out of my folio, so she knew I meant business.

I'd brought a bottle of water in my bag, but then I became too concerned my bag looked like a purse, and I'd left the whole thing outside at the front desk. The only thing I'd brought with me was a digital recorder that the State Department lackey gave me back at the guesthouse, to record her confession.

None of this made any sense.

"Do you know why I'm here?" I wasn't being coy. It was written right there in the script. For some reason, US government officials trying to extradite known criminals overseas had to ask *them* if *they* knew what was going on.

"Do *you* know why you're here?" She kept her gaze down, and I was so relieved. If she looked at me, I didn't know what I would do. Probably shit myself. I hadn't eaten all day to try and preclude this possibility.

She had a point. I didn't know why I was there. But luckily there was the script, so I could press forward and not inhibit the interview by admitting that I, in fact, had no idea.

"I'm with the FDA. I'm here to take your statement in response to charges the American government intends to file against you that will result in your extradition to the United States, where your case will be heard and prosecuted to the fullest extent of the law. Do you have any questions for me before we get started?"

"I have none." She had a bandage on her upper arm, I noticed. Had she gotten that in jail? What got her captured? Unlike her, I had so many questions. I went back to the script.

"Kwa Lele Odoki, you are being charged with these crimes under United States Food and Drug Laws, United States Trade Laws, the Food and Drug Safety Act of 1960, the Extradition Treaty of the International Criminal Court of 1995—"

"The United States is neither a signatory nor a supporter of the International Criminal Court," she said, and she had me there.

"—and the 2001 Extradition Treaty Between The United States and South Africa. In the absence of a valid and binding extradition treaty between South Africa and the requesting State, the sought person can still be extradited to the requesting state."

I licked the driest lips with the driest tongue and continued.

"South Africa's Extradition Act provides in section 3(2) that a person is liable for extradition, even when no extradition treaty with the requesting state exists, if the president in writing consents to that person's surrender. Extradition from South Africa in the absence of a binding operative extradition treaty has been considered and accepted as constitutionally valid by the Constitutional Court. But in this case, the Extradition Treaty exists and is binding in this case."

The script was very repetitive.

"I would like to bring a case of my own," Kwa Lele Odoki said.

"Uh," I said. The script didn't address this situation. "What is the, uh, nature of your, um, case."

"That I have been framed for these crimes."

"You aren't the leader of a, uh, militia that is funded by...by—"

"I am the leader of the fiercest militia this world has ever seen. Do we visit swift and merciless justice to those who have beaten women, who have raped, who have enslaved others? Yes.

But I do not use funding from false drugs of men so they can lift their limp penises. This accusation is a trap."

"What do you mean, a trap?"

"Why would they send a know-nothing fool to interview me?"

Kwa Lele snapped. "They are not framing only me, James Schneider. They are framing you too. Now we are both on the gallows."

"Why would they be framing me? Who's they?"

"Who knows you are here? Your wife? Your children?"

I looked down. I heard her shackles rattle closer. She leaned forward. I could barely look at her. Was she going to die in America? Who would frame her, or me?

"No. I don't have a wife and children. I—I used to," I said.

"And?" I tried to meet Kwa Lele Odoki's eyes, but I couldn't. I stared at her nose instead.

"But my wife had an operation after our child was born. To repair her pelvis. They put some bad medical device in her, and it drove her insane. She killed herself. Before she killed herself, she drowned our children in the bathtub."

"And what did you do?"

"What do you mean?"

"Where were you?"

"I was there all along. I didn't do anything to stop it. I didn't even listen to her complaints, really. It was right in front of my face, all the pain. She was losing her mind. I minimized it all. I worked for the FDA then, too. It would have been so easy for me to access the medical device database and see the lawsuits. But I didn't."

I looked into her eyes then, I don't know why. Glutton for punishment, that's me. I wanted to see her disgust, I suppose. She didn't look like a prisoner. Her eyes were so defiant.

I was shocked to see she didn't pity me at all.

I had never said any of that out loud to anybody. And I'd also, never, *not* been pitied, almost immediately, by everybody who met me.

"Listen," I said. "Maybe I can help—"

Kwa Lele's hair was divided into a hundred braids that streamed down the center of her back. Her skin looked so smooth. I was nervous to look at her. I wanted to touch her hand and tell her it was going to be okay. I had never done that for anybody, lied to them about things being okay. Of course it wasn't. Nothing was ever okay.

A distant rumbling sound outside started from nothing and became a roar in my ears in seconds flat.

She and I looked up. Only I was surprised. She had been expecting this all along.

The corners of her mouth twitched.

Her cell's lone window shattered. I leapt up to run, but then I hesitated, looked back at her. The outer wall imploded.

Sharp heat and rubble engulfed me. My face was hot, the smoke was everywhere. I was on the ground already. I scrambled to pull myself up, but my arm collapsed. Only one eye could open, saw bone poking up through the flesh on my right wrist. My hand was still there, but I couldn't feel it. My eardrums whined. I touched my ear and blood flowed from it. Distant screaming.

It was me, I was screaming.

The walls kept falling staccato blasts all around, some flashes through the smoke. The dust was settling.

My leg was trapped. I tried to pull forward to get away from the heat, but my skin tore. I was going to die.

The pressure lifted, then, from my ankle.

"Get up!" Kwa Lele shouted.

"I can't!"

Her eyes, so furious. She yanked me up out of the debris like a blubbering infant. I screamed with the pain in both my legs. Also like an infant, I couldn't walk. I tottered over. I blacked out.

I woke to the statue of Nelson Mandela, smiling down upon me, on my back in the rubble.

"Mr. Schneider." One of the guards. Her face was cut and bleeding, but the rest of her was completely intact. The only female guard.

"What happened—" I lost the ability to speak before I could say another word. My lungs were on fire.

"Kwa Lele Odoki has escaped. It was the Women's Liberation Army."

"Where's the...?"

"He's dead. Most of the other staff members were killed."

I heard sirens in the distance.

Kwa Lele rising out of the dust, pulling me up out of the rubble.
Was that real, or did I imagine it?

My arm moved on its own, jumped up and down, jerky movements I couldn't control, I panted for breath, I couldn't catch my
breath, my lungs were burning, my arm, my chest vibrated all on
their own for no reason. I tried to hold still. I couldn't hold myself
still. I couldn't get up off the ground and I couldn't stay still.

"Are you okay?" The guard.

"I don't know," I said. "I don't know what's happening."

"Help is coming."

"I don't know," I said again. I had to stay awake.

I closed my one good eye.

Still so bright it was like I hadn't even shut it at all.

25

I WOKE UP

I woke up in a hospital bed. Institutional paneling in the ceiling. I stared at it. Just like work. College. Grade school. Ceiling panels the same the world over. Why did this crumbly, depressing, ceiling tile take over the world?

I couldn't turn my head because I couldn't move, thanks to a complex system of body part casts, tubes hooked to machines, pulleys and levers and straps, sensors and wires.

I was ceiling tiles' captive audience.

My whole body was on fire. Did they have opioids in South Africa? If so, they hadn't administered them to me.

I looked for a call button. Nothing.

I waited.

The pain ratcheted up. It shot down from my hand and ran up my arm. My head started to throb. My face was numb on the left side. That was what inspired the terror to creep in: the parts of my body I couldn't feel at all.

"Nurse?" I rasped.

I was alone in the room. The sun was shining outside. It hurt my eye. I opened my right eye under its bandage. Could it still see?

"Hello?" I called louder.

Nothing.

"*Hello?*" Elise calling out from the darkened bedroom, 3 am. I was on the couch. We'd had a fight, she threw me out, that was around 11 pm. I chalked it up to a hormonal imbalance. Elise didn't have to work. She could focus exclusively on raising the kids. I brought home a paycheck, paid the bills. I was *involved*. I was a good husband, father. Her pain, was it for attention? That's what everybody was implying. The doctors couldn't find anything wrong.

Pain for attention.

Had I ever been accused of that?

"Good morning, Mr. Schneider. How are you feeling today?"

Oh, thank you. Finally. I opened my good eye back up.

"Like a wall fell on me."

"We'll have you back on your feet soon enough." Not a doctor. The attendant wheeled over a narrow shelf meant to accommodate my extensive network of health accessories, and slid a tray of food onto it.

"Please send a nurse or a doctor. I need something for the pain."

I wedged a fork into my good hand, stabbed a block of feta atop a raw onion ring, and then gave up completely. What explosion survivor ever looked at a raw onion ring seated atop a pile of largely chunked salad upon awakening and thought, Oh good. This is exactly why I survived. To experience the joy of eating uncooked vegetables.

Tell me. Name one.

My whole body throbbed.

I thought about her again to distract myself. Every time I did, my heart monitor increased its pace. Besides the pain, I could do nothing but think of her.

Or, I wanted to do nothing but think of her.

"Jim. You're awake." A guy in a suit burst in. I could tell by his callous expression he was with the US government.

"Who the hell are you?"

A doctor entered, flanked by a couple of others.

"Mr. Schneider. You're lucky to be alive. How'd you manage to escape?"

"Good question," the guy in the suit echoed. Trimmed beard. Gelled hair. I wanted to flop out of my bed and murder him.

"Are you family?" the doctor asked.

"Yes," he said.

"No, he's not," I rasped. "Get him out of here."

"Oh, Jim, you don't mean that. You're going to want to hear what I have to say. I'll come back another time. I can see you're indisposed."

I glared at him. "Are you with the FDA?"

"I'm not. I'll see you later, buddy."

Buddy.

The doctor ran down a list of my injuries: compound fracture, right wrist. Eye contusion. Concussion. Possible brain swelling. Some internal damage on my left side, leading to enlarged spleen, possibility of required surgery. Broken femur, left leg. Some burns. I inhaled a lot of dust. May have seared my lungs. They were still running tests and had to put me back through the scanner later that day.

"I need something for the pain. Please."

The doctor nodded, and soon the staff had set up another intravenous drip. After that I was in a beautiful haze. I focused my attention back on Kwa Lele. She had saved me, I knew. I knew it wasn't a dream.

"I'M NOT SAYING you contributed to her escape," John from the State Department said, again, in the most offensive tone. "I just need to take a statement from you about the incident."

"Talk to my lawyer," I said.

"Oh, have you hired a lawyer?" He raised his eyebrows at me, unbuttoned the cuff of one sleeve of his shirt, and made a big show of rolling it up. I still couldn't make any sudden movements without the sweet drip of generic morphine.

"No," I said. "If I did, would you stop visiting me?"

He was cutting into my Kwa Lele imagining time. In today's

scenario, we lived in a tiny A-frame in the Catskills, had no friends, and no family, and spent most of our time watching sitcoms together. Which is exactly what a militia leader would want for herself.

John from the State Department moved the room's lone chair from over by the window so he could sit right next to my face.

"Listen, Jim. Help me help you."

"John, you listen. Help you help me get you out of here."

"If I put, 'no statement' down on the report, it's going to open a whole can of worms."

"For you or for me? I'm in an elaborate series of casts. Can's open. My worms are out."

The doctor entered, entourage of two.

John nodded at him. He nodded at John.

"A little privacy, here?" I pushed my morphine button, responding to a fire deep in my shoulder. "He's not family," I said to the doctor. "Nor a friend."

"I could be," John said. "But you're right. I'm not."

26

I STUMBLED OFF

I stumbled off the plane, struggling to manage my carry on with my one good arm. Nobody offered to help me. Nobody even looked at me. It was clear that I was back in the United States.

You have two masses, the doctor had said. One near your heart, and one in your stomach. He pointed them out on the scan: two shadows in my body. We recommend you seek treatment as soon as you get home.

The sterile international arrivals wing of Dulles made me feel ill. What was I doing here? I didn't have to come back to America to convalesce if I could struggle out of the plane with my own suitcase. Where did I want to go, then? Back to Afghanistan?

I wanted to get in touch with Kwa Lele, is what I really wanted to do. But I had no idea *how*. Did the leaders of female militias have email?

Twitter, perhaps?

"Thumb, please," The customs official said. I put my thumb down on the glass, and grimaced. Pain rang all the way up and down my arm.

"To the left," he said.

I moved my thumb to the left.

"Flatten."

I flattened and gasped.

"Now you're off the screen. More to the right."

I edged my thumb to the right.

"Again," he said.

I moved more to the right.

"No, flatten," he said.

"Would it be easier if I took the thumb off and gave it to you," I said. "Because I could."

The man looked up and through me, letting me know I'd not brightened his day with my humor.

"I'm an American citizen."

"I'm afraid saying so isn't sufficient for entry, sir. Please flatten," he said.

I flattened.

———————

I SWIPED my card and the red light flashed. Uh-oh. First the country, now my office.

"I'm Jim. Jim Schneider," I said. "I've worked here for 12 years."

"Looks like your card is expired, Mr. Schneider," the guard said.

"It shouldn't be," I said. "I've been working non-stop in Afghanistan for 6 months."

"Afghanistan." The guy laughed. "What are you doing there? Nothing but desert and explosions as far as the eye can see. I was in Afghanistan back in 2001."

"We're opening a branch of foreign posts there," I said. Maybe I shouldn't be telling him this, I thought. Was it classified? There was no such thing as classified at the FDA.

There were only trade secrets, privileged or confidential information. Intellectual property. Patents. Trademarks.

Well, nothing that they admitted was classified.

He looked me up and down.

"They still feeding you pecan pie at the compound?"

"Every day," I said. I pointed at my stomach. He nodded and handed me back my card.

"Good stuff," he said.

I couldn't get it into the slot. I swiped it in front of and behind the reader. A little to the left, then the right. Bent it towards the sensor. Took a deep breath. Why was everything this hard? Finally made a connection. There was a beep of recognition. The red light flashed again.

I dropped my card on the ground.

The guard hit a button and opened the gate manually.

I braced myself to bend over, which took no fewer than fifteen minutes and a complex set of movements and gestures across my still-broken and now potentially tumor-ridden body.

"Go on ahead, Mr. Schneider. Thank you for your service," he said. He ran out and picked my card up off the ground, handed it to me.

What service? So far, I hadn't served anything or anybody.

TIME TO SORT through the 7,632 emails I'd received in one month of hospital stay.

I scrolled. Mostly junk. Then I saw one real email, from Ravi. I hadn't thought about him in the hospital more than once or twice, him and Rahim. The inspections. The carpet bomb. Whatever had happened. However it had turned out. A flaming pile of charred bodies. Or not.

Then another email from him, and another. About a week old. I did a search by sender: in total, there were fifty-six emails from Ravi.

SUBJECT: A lot of new weirdos around
   Subject: I can't believe they sent you to South Africa
   Subject: Nobody's getting carpet bombed
   Subject: Maybe I'm getting carpet bombed

Subject: How's it going over there
Subject: These miners are hella blond
Subject: no subject
Subject: no subject
Subject: I need you to call me as soon as you can
Subject: I'm heading back to the US
Subject: no subject
Subject: no subject

THAT WAS THE FIRST PAGE. There were four more.

I called his phone. It went right to voicemail.

Maybe he was back already and at his Rockville office? I checked the date on that email. A couple of weeks ago. I wandered out into the hallway, considered getting in my car and driving over there, when Jane Foxhall intercepted me in the second-floor walkway between Buildings 31 and 32.

I'd forgotten Jane Foxhall even existed.

"Oh, Jim. How are you feeling? Terrible about Ravi." Jane's perfectly coiffed curls bobbed when she shook her head back and forth.

"What do you mean?" I stopped walking and I stopped breathing. "Did something happen?"

"Oh, I'm so sorry." She touched my elbow. "I thought you knew. Not in Afghanistan. He was back. Unfortunate incident last weekend, on the Waterfront. Terrible. Freak accident. Devastating. His wife and kids." Jane masked her mouth with one manicured hand and sighed through it.

When's the last time you got home from Afghanistan and decided to go sailing, alone?

In Washington, DC.

"The funeral is Saturday," she said. "There's an announcement in your emails. I have to run to a meeting now." She put her hand on my unsplinted forearm. "Please contact Staff Care and talk to somebody about all this. You've had a rough month."

"Thanks," I said. "Maybe I will." I nodded.

As soon as her back was turned, I shuffle-loped back to my office. I banged my pin code into my computer's home screen, getting it wrong the first time, as ever, slamming the mouse around with my good hand as if it would call up Ravi's emails any faster.

I clicked my email open, panting like an Ironman triathlete in the final stretch instead of a guy who'd lightly scuffed down a very short corridor.

They were gone. Every single one of fifty-six emails Ravi had sent me in the past month had disappeared from my inbox. While I was talking to Jane Foxhall. The fluorescent light directly overhead flickered.

27

WE STOOD AROUND

We stood around a rectangular hole in the ground at Gates of Heaven Cemetery. I'd assumed they were Hindus. The service was Episcopalian. It wasn't comforting in any way, identical in that respect to Elise's funeral. Cold, sterile, joyless and void of despair, except what you brought within you and hid. Rituals in America were shit, I now knew after only a few months elsewhere. Total shit. Just a business transaction.

I'd arrived late, and as a third-tier guest, I had to stand. They'd run out of chairs. Ravi was beloved.

I had to talk to Ravi's wife. Did Pritya know what happened to her husband?

What did the missing emails mean? What had they said? Pritya was the only person who might have the slightest clue what Ravi was doing before his death. I strained to pick her out. There she was, bending down to wipe something off Naveen's face while she spoke to the other little one. I couldn't remember their daughter's name.

It was a gray day, like it had been at Elise's funeral. Hers was on the other side of Silver Spring, though, in the other cemetery.

The minister invited us to sit back down. That didn't apply to me. I shuffled from one foot to the other. Standing was better for me now anyway. I could feel the oxycodone wearing off. Pritya's shoulders shook. She hoisted the little girl whose name I couldn't remember up into her lap, and covered the tiny hands with her own.

BACK AT THEIR HOME, I steeled myself. It was now or never.

"Pritya? I'm—"

"Jim, I know who you are. You've eaten at this table before."

She stepped forward to hug me, stumbled over an end table, and fell onto my bad arm. I yelped involuntarily.

"I'm sorry," I said. She tore apart a recent injury and *I* apologized. "I know you know me. It's just, it's been so long." Ravi and I had spent quite a bit of time together in those early days, but after Elise got sick I had fallen off completely.

"I spent so many sleepless nights while you two were in Afghanistan. When Ravi was coming home, I thanked God he was returned to me safely."

"I know, Pritya. I'm so sorry." I was sorry about Ravi. Sorry, and wanted answers. "What...happened? Did he say where he was going when he..."

But what would I do with the answers when I got them?

"Punam," Naveen shouted. He'd been displeased, somehow, by his younger sister. He shoved her off the area rug by the sofa. She toddled over and tugged at her mom's skirt. That was her name. Punam. Unborn when Ravi and I first met. Only Naveen back then. He was still a little dictator.

"Mommy." Pritya picked her up and held her close. I didn't want to say anything else in front of the children.

She kissed Punam on the cheek and handed her to a nearby relative.

"Mommy is coming, darling. Go be with Aunty Mitzy for a few minutes while I talk to daddy's friend."

"When is daddy coming back?"

"Daddy is in heaven, sweetie."

"Why?"

"Because that's where good people go when they die."

"I wish I had died in childbirth." One of many sentences Elise spoke to me directly to let me know something was very, very wrong. What if she had? I imagined it every day for the first nine months after she took matters into her own hands. I pictured myself caring for them, comforting them. Being the most amazing single father widower.

Pure fantasy. Had I changed a diaper? Even given them a bath without Elise's careful supervision? I couldn't recall.

Pritya steered me away from the crowd and into a study. Ravi's study. It was lined with biomedical textbooks, binder after binder of his research documentation. Would there be a clue in here? I wouldn't even know what the hell I was looking at. I was the wrong man for this investigation. For any investigation.

"Tell me, Jim, was Ravi doing something illegal?"

"Pritya, no. God, no. Well. I don't think so. It was a gray area. I don't know exactly what he was doing. We had only recently connected. I hadn't seen him in years, since..."

She nodded, so I didn't have to say it.

"He was doing research down at the FDA, clinical trials."

"Yes. The fat rats."

So she knew that much. How many people had Ravi told about his *secret* research for the CIA?

"Ravi was out of sorts when he got back from Afghanistan. He didn't tell me why. I thought it was shock. I asked him if anything bad happened there, if he was in an explosion or saw some violence. He said no, but he was shaken. I could tell. The night he died, he said he had to go meet somebody. I was distracted with the kids. I didn't think twice about it. I was just so glad he was back home. It never occurred to me that he could..."

"Where did he go?"

"He met someone down on the Waterfront. They found his body there, on the steps that lead down to the water, by the marina, and all the restaurants. The police said it looked like he slipped, hit his head, fell in, and drowned."

"Bullshit," I said.

"That's what I think, too," she said. "They said the autopsy supported it, and there were no eyewitnesses. Nobody saw anything at 9 pm on the Waterfront on Saturday? There are a hundred restaurants down there. People live on those boats. Wouldn't somebody have seen something?"

"Can you get an independent autopsy?"

Listen to me, using my extensive working knowledge of postmortem possibilities learned from the many flavors of *Law and Order.*

"Two of Ravi's cousins are lawyers. They're somewhere around here," she said, searching the crowd that had invaded her home. Dozens of people, maybe more than a hundred, snacking. "We're planning to sit down together to discuss it. I don't know what to do. It's like a nightmare."

If I were more of a human, I would have overcome my own physical pain to put my hand on hers. Instead, I said:

"Did he say who he was going to meet?"

"Ravi called out a name before he left. I didn't hear the first name. The last name sounded Irish to me. Started with an O. O'Dacchy?"

My heart clenched. I felt dizzy.

"Odoki?" I breathed.

"Yes," she said. One tear spilled over, soaked into her funeral blouse. "Do you know him?"

I SAT in the car and stared straight ahead. I couldn't think. A Lexus LC 500 pulled up behind me. A familiar slick, black-pantsuited figure emerged. Had Jane even known Ravi? I slouched down, trying to remain undetected, but she picked me out immediately and stalked up to my driver side, trapped me into conversation in my own car.

I rolled down the car window.

"How are you, Jim? I wanted to come pay my respects to Pritya. On behalf of all of us at the FDA."

Guess she knew Ravi's wife. Jane Foxhall and Ravi must have been acquainted with each other, too.

"I'm okay, Jane."

"Good. You've been through a lot. If you want to take some time for yourself before you come back to work, we'll understand. Call Staff Care."

"I will, Jane. Thanks."

I finally exhaled when she stepped back from my window and I could pull away from the house. But where to?

I'd promised Pritya I would do everything I could, but as usual, everything I could do was a veritable nothing. I reviewed what I knew.

Ravi was contracted by the CIA to study Mineral X. Contracted wasn't the right word. He was a federal employee. Compelled, was more like it.

Forced.

Assigned.

He may have blown up his own laboratory.

Question mark on that one: He may have blown up his own laboratory? Seems far-fetched, but I saw what I saw. He fled the site of his own exploded laboratory, somehow escaping seconds before the blast, and that was the truth.

Whatever Ravi knew, he was valuable enough to ship to Afghanistan.

He saw something there, *56 emails* worth of something.

Either he returned, or he *was* returned.

Then he was murdered.

I found myself hitting 495 towards the Waterfront. I didn't know what I possibly could find down there, but it was the only way I could feel like I wasn't failing Ravi.

Murdered upon return by Kwa Lele?

Kwa Lele claimed she was being framed. Didn't most criminals assert their own innocence? Was she a murderer? How had she even gotten to the United States? She controlled a female army that had successfully busted her out of jail. They could have run her in circles around the Earth ten times before the FDA could get me one contract flight for domestic travel.

A light rain got harder. I flicked the wipers on with my damaged hand, screamed a little, rooted around blindly on the seat next to me for my pills. Knocked the bottle onto the floor, and got spooked by how sparse the rattle sounded.

I needed a refill on my prescription. I was taking too many pills. I needed them. I needed them now.

I also needed to believe she was innocent. I didn't know why, I just did.

I LURKED out in front of Hank's Oyster Bar, staring at the steps Ravi allegedly tripped down, cracked his head open on, and suffered a traumatic brain injury, unwitnessed on the busiest promenade in all of Washington DC on primetime Saturday night. DC wasn't a raging party city full of the energy of, say, New York or Los Angeles, but there were restaurants all along the walkway. There was no way to have an unnoticed slip-and-fall accident.

I studied all the boats parked in their slips. Someone could have easily escaped onto one of those. But again, wouldn't someone have seen? Maybe I could get a closer look at the boats. I walked the ramp, but there was a gate with a key-FOB entry to keep boatless losers like myself out.

If it *was* murder, though, regardless of the perpetrator, why wouldn't there be some mention? I flipped through every search result on my phone. Nothing. Newspapers love reporting on murders. Even and especially the speculative.

I paced up one side of the pedestrian walkway and down the other. It was a fruitless endeavor. I turned down a side-street to head back to my car, when a strong arm grabbed my recently assembled shoulder and pressed me up against the wall.

Kwa Lele Odoki and I were face to face again.

In all the times I'd imagined this happening, I was not crying from pain she was inflicting on my broken body.

She released me, and watched me.

As breathtaking as she had been in the jail cell. She'd shorn her hair off, nearly to the scalp. She was wearing jeans and a t-shirt. Blending in with Americans perfectly except for the brilliant defiance in her eyes and the way she'd thrown me up against a wall.

"Are you here to kill me too?" I stammered out. "After you saved me in the jail? You could have left me there and saved yourself the trip."

"Shut up, you fool," she hissed. "We have to get out of here. You're being followed."

"By who?"

"Probably some Jane Foxhall hire."

Jane Foxhall.

"Jane Foxhall?"

Kwa Lele nodded. "Follow me," she whispered. "Don't say another word."

We silently strode out from the alley. When we hit the main pedestrian walkway, Kwa Lele took my hand in hers, as if we were lovers out for a stroll, instead of an international criminal and a government worker fleeing from a multinational crime syndicate that extended to the uppermost levels of the US government, among others.

Like Sweden.

And South Africa.

And Afghanistan.

She pasted a fake smile on and I did the same. She tilted her head towards me, as if to kiss me on the cheek, and said,

"Those two men down on the waterfront steps, they're here to kill you."

I glanced over her shoulder to see a couple of men scanning the pedestrian walkway. Glasses. Overcoats. Guns would account for the bulk. But what would they do, shoot us in public?

"What are they going to do? Shoot us in front of all these people?"

"Yes," she said. "You *fool*. Why did you come here? That is exactly what they are going to do if they catch us together. The back story is that I am the leader of a terrorist organization and you aided and abetted my escape. One of these things is true. We are both guilty of many other crimes by now. Human trafficking, extortion, fraud. They'll say we shot first, and then they will throw guns on top of our dead bodies."

I imagined my picture on the cover of the Post until Kwa Lele jerked my arm and I gasped, and she led me away from my own death.

"THIS IS HOW YOU GOT HERE?" I must have asked that a dozen times. I couldn't believe it was possible to cross an ocean in such a tiny piece of junk boat. We were below deck on the Solanum incanum, Kwa Lele in the galley, me seated on the bed in the main bedroom— though I could have reached out and touched her graceful leg, the boat was so tiny.

"Don't you worry about it," the First Mate said. She would have been intimidating even had she not been in a militia, for her height, and her ship captain uniform, and for an explosive vegetable-chopping method. Right now, she was dicing vegetables for our would-be dinner, while Kwa Lele busied herself around the ship, either tying a complicated-looking knot or wrestling an impossibly sharp object into its designated spot. With those two pairs of hands at work, I could have easily been choked dead a dozen times already.

"How did you think the wanted leader of an illicit militia traveled?" The ship mechanic asked. "American Airlines?" She hauled open a panel in the floor and disappeared into it. I might have been better off with the lazier murderers outside.

We were hidden in plain sight, one row over from our would-be killers. Kwa Lele and her colleagues had taken up residence in the very marina where Ravi had been killed.

Not exactly reassuring, but not evidence one way or the other, I supposed.

"Do you ever think about quitting the militia life and, you know, settling down?"

Kwa Lele stood up her full length, head nearly touching the galley ceiling.

"When I was a girl of eleven or twelve—I never knew my real age —the military came out to our village to put down the rebel insurrection. Rebels. Ha. We were very poor villagers. We had no stakes to claim, we knew nothing of the diamonds, or anything else they stole out of the ground, we were unarmed. Still, they came out to hack off the limbs of the men, and while they were there, they raped the women, and children. Children like me.

Three of the soldiers came into our house. They said my father was a rebel. My mother and my brother were away that day, in the next town over.

I was there all alone.

After they were done, two of them went outside. The third one, he had a petrol can. He shook petrol on my body, to light me on fire. I was broken, all over. I did not think I could move. But I did. I got up. And I reached up my hand, so quick. And I grabbed, and I started pulling, and pulling. I tore until that man's body part came off in my hand. I didn't feel him when he struck me. I tore him apart with my child's hands.

He beat me until I vomited blood.

That wasn't even the worst of my young life.

I didn't look for that fight. Fighting found me."

Kwa Lele looked level at me. I imagined taking her into my arms and comforting her, but she would hate it, and probably try to kill me. I ventured to reach out my hand and put it on her hand, but I only made it halfway before I chickened out.

"I'm sorry," I said. I hated myself instantly for apologizing to her for her own tragedy, like all those morons who apologized to me when my family died. "No, that's too small a phrase for what you went through," I said. "What I meant to say was, I'm glad you tore off that guy's penis."

Kwa Lele's smile was a twitch at the right corner of her mouth. "I wish I had kept that courage," she said.

"Didn't you?"

She didn't respond.

"What does your militia do?"

"All the things that governments, and the police, won't." Her first mate said, every other word a knife-chop. She finished by hammering the butcher's knife into the chopping block so hard, it stuck, and the heel of the zucchini ricocheted off the ceiling.

"We rescued two hundred and sixty-six kidnapped girls from Boko Haram a couple of months ago. That was my favorite mission so far," Kwa Lele said. She coiled a rope and tucked it into a hole in the wall.

"Nobody else would have done it," the mechanic, now filth-coated, lifted herself out of the engine room, chimed in. Grabbed a rag off a clip on the wall, wiped her oily hands on both sides.

"No and no, that was certain. The authorities wanted to wait until all those girls had been violated thousands of times. We had to act."

"Sometimes violence can be the best method of communication," the first mate and the mechanic intoned in unison.

"Sometimes violence can be the best method of communication," Kwa Lele agreed. She rose from her seat, opened their tiny refrigerator, and removed a bottle. "Fizzy water?" She asked me.

"Yes, please," I said.

She bottle-opened and handed me one. The rain hit harder above deck. I was momentarily happy about our wannabe killers getting wet, hopefully dying of pneumonia and solving a couple of problems right then and there. Then my pain surged and I couldn't be happy about anything anymore.

"Are you quite alright?" Kwa Lele asked.

"No," I said. "You blew me up. Or, one of you did."

"Yes," she said. "We all did. But then I pulled you out and dusted you off." The corner of her mouth twitched, and mine did too. I would endure a lifetime of oxycodone addiction, and that was for sure what I was embarking on, if I lasted another day or another week besides, if it meant Kwa Lele almost smiled.

"How are you mixed up in this FDA stuff?" I asked.

The upturned corner of her mouth sank. There was a noise outside. Kwa Lele's head whipped around. She tracked it until the noise faded, eyes narrowed, and then she relaxed.

"I was framed," she said.

"By who?"

"By the man who raped me as a child for twelve years. It's his revenge for my escape."

"*He* raped *you*, and *he's* getting—" The words died in my mouth. Restating injustice as if it was abnormal was the equivalent of apologizing for your wife killing your kids, then herself. "Who is he?"

"Paul Tussey," she said. "He used to be a Director for the UN, worked at Bidi Bidi. Now he's consulting for the State Department."

"Paul," I said.

"You know him?" She eyed me.

"Not well." I didn't want her to be suspicious. "He briefed me when I first got to Afghanistan."

"I bet he did," Kwa Lele said. "He's eliminating me. By framing me. I guess the question for you is, what did you do to get on the hit list? Did he rape you as a child too?"

I had nothing to say. I really didn't know. He hadn't.

"I don't think Paul is even my top murder suspect," I said. "I don't know how we get out of this."

"The only way out is through," she said. It sounded very zen, but I didn't know what the hell it meant.

"Did you kill Ravi?" I asked.

She nodded, and sipped on her fizzy water. "Gutted him like a grouper." She didn't blink. The first mate was enacting that task over at the galley counter.

"The police reports said he hit his head," I said.

"The police lie," Kwa Lele said.

"Jim," the first mate slid the grouper's guts into the sink. "Have you ever entered a hostile territory with your elite trained unit of freedom fighting women for the purpose of forced stabilization in the face of the enemy?"

"No," I said. "I can't say that I have. I've never even touched a gun."

"Then who said you could ask any questions at all?"

"He was my friend," I said.

Kwa Lele looked at me a long time.

"What did Jane Foxhall say?"

"Do you know Jane?" Kwa Lele didn't answer. She didn't have to. It was a dumb question. I heard the stupidity as soon as it passed my lips. "She said I can go back to Afghanistan whenever I feel ready. Resume work."

"I think that's the best course of action. Don't you?"

I didn't, actually. I wanted the best course of action to be her, somehow. Her, being near me. She must have seen me, wanting this, because she said:

"If we get caught together by these henchmen outside, we die. You have to go back, Jim. Back to Afghanistan. It's the safest thing for you, for...everyone." I didn't care about everyone. I didn't care about *anyone*. Only Kwa Lele.

"My flight's already booked," I said. It wasn't.

The first mate beheaded the grouper with one crack of the cleaver. "This is the best part of the fish," she said.

Kwa Lele was too busy fighting for justice to sit on a couch in an A-frame in the Catskills and watch sitcoms with me, anyway. Once I lost my job at the FDA, I wouldn't even be able to offer her that much.

"But these jerks, and whatever network of monsters they belong to..." I flung my hand out, towards where I thought our would-be attackers stood watch. "...you think they'll let me waltz in, again? Back into Afghanistan?"

"I think that's right where they want you," Kwa Lele nodded grimly. "And as long as we remain apart, we might live to see another day. Once we're spotted together, that's it." She drew her finger across her stunning neck.

I said, "Alright. I'll go back."

The first mate wrapped up her grouper work and popped the whole thing inside the galley oven. That must be how ships catch on fire. Elaborate, slow-cooked meals.

The women seemed content to sit in silence while we listened to the grouper sizzle, but I had to ruin it with:

"I just don't know how to get past these two goons waiting for us outside."

"We set sail twenty minutes ago," the first mate said.

"What?"

"We're asea," Kwa Lele said.

"Where are we going?" I cried. I opened the ratty porthole curtain, tearing it along the way. "Sorry," I muttered under my breath.

Sure enough. Nothing but ocean out there, whipped by rain.

I was exaggerating. I could easily recognize the Arlington skyline. We weren't far from our point of origin.

"We're dropping you off at an inlet close to your home," Kwa Lele said.

"What about my car?"

Kwa Lele looked at me like I was a mosquito. "Uber."

"You must be really high," the first mate said.

"I've had more sober times in my life," I said. Then I fished my oxycodone bottle out and dry-swallowed another one, judged hard by the double-stare of the leadership coalition of a women's militia.

28

THIS TIME, I

This time, I entered Kabul with ease. I traveled light, doped up on pills. I veritably skipped off the plane when we arrived, and I turned a hard left on the walkway to sit in the armored car on the pavement, to wait for the other invading forces, to skip the airport terminal, to take my helicopter ride to the embassy compound.

I looked down on Kabul, hat-free so as to not kill us all on the chopper. The river that wound its way around town was a deep shade of purple these days, I noted.

"Jim, who signed off on all the inspection activities?" Diane stood up and threw back her chair, exasperated with my inability to connect the dots.

"Technically..."

"Who?"

"I did."

"Why did they send you to interview a renegade militia leader?"

"She was in the FDA's top ten most wanted. They said they didn't have anybody else in-country."

"Bullshit. They couldn't have sent anybody else? Anybody stationed there with the State Department? Any other member of law enforcement?"

I moved as little as possible while still conveying my shrug.

"Any other human body?" Diane's voice was getting that same shrill edge to it she'd gotten about an hour ago, when I screwed up while trying to manipulate her vagina in a way I thought she should enjoy. Disappointment growing. Patience running out.

"They're connecting Kwa Lele's so-called money laundering from fake drug sales to the cartels in Afghanistan. And there's only one other connection."

I stared at her blankly.

I knew whatever she was saying, she was basically right, but I was in my newly-swallowed oxycodone fugue, and my reaction time was even slower than usual.

Listening comprehension, nil.

"You. It's you, you idiot. They're setting *you* up. They're trying to make it look like you have a connection to her, like you both are leading this international crime ring."

"Who?"

"Paul and Polly. Paul and Polly! Fucking Paul and fucking Polly! How many fucking times do I have to spell this out?"

"Why me?"

"Why *you*? Why *not* you? Who are you, again? Oh, a nobody low-level government worker with absolutely no connections, friends, family? Not even any colleagues who know you?"

"I had one, but they—"

"You could be the next Sirhan Sirhan. You're perfect! Paul and Polly are framing both of you, *her* and *you*. You're their scapegoat. This makes it an inside job. The investigation can take years. It's all smoke and mirrors."

"What about her?"

"Who? Kwa Lele?"

"Yes, why would they do this to her? All part of the conspiracy?" I air-quoted conspiracy and I thought Diane was going to deck me. "Sorry," I said. "I don't even know why I did that."

"It's not a conspiracy, Jim. Just Cold War business as usual."

"Russia Cold War, Diane? Or Swedish?"

"What do you know about the Swedes?"

"Nothing, except what you told me. And then I met one down at the delegation. Can't remember her name. Long neck."

"Lanna Bergström."

"Who is she? Kwa Lele."

"We were talking about Lanna Bergström."

"Yeah but that's not who I'm getting co-framed with. What do you know about Kwa Lele Odoki?"

"You can't focus on *shit* while you're all hopped up on these pills." Diane said, sighing. "I don't know too much about her. They say that she was born into a refugee camp, and that one of the aid workers... molested her. Repeatedly."

"Disgusting."

"Worse than disgusting. She was just a child. One of the other employees found out, so this aid worker, pretty high up guy, I guess, had her transferred to another camp. And then he moved there himself so he could go on raping her."

"And nobody stopped it?"

"Who's going to? Another refugee, stuck in a camp, unable to travel anywhere or escape, relying on that child molester for food? Who do you report it to? The UN? He *was* the UN. What's a child refugee supposed to do? File a lawsuit?" Diane snorted.

"But eventually she got out—"

"She fled to Europe, after years of abuse. That's all I know about her. The charges claim her organization created shell institutions in order to receive funding from someone within USAID."

"A lot of funding?"

"Yeah, a lot of funding. Two hundred and fifty million dollars over ten years. It's how the militia funds itself. Weapons, vehicles, planes, bribes. Also, real businesses, grants, non-profit organizations. It's a complex web of legal and illegal."

"If they've got all that funding, what do they need with fake Viagra?"

"I think it's a bullshit story. They needed it to get the FDA involved. They needed it to link her to you."

"Why didn't they just kill me when I was back in the United States?"

"Why kill somebody in the United States when you can blow them up with a shitty pipe bomb in Afghanistan, save yourself some money on bullets, and blame the terrorists for the whole thing?"

It *did* sound very efficient, and nicely cost effective, when she said it like that. I was gonna die at the hands of some career bureaucrats who really snip-snipped their way through all that red tape to murder me. I put my head down on the pillow.

"You have to stop taking this shit," Diane said, and I heard my beautiful pills rattle into the trashcan in Diane's bathroom. "You're so high you may as well be dead already." I vowed to fish them out when I woke up.

29

I YAWNED AND

I yawned and stretched. One thing about the climate of Afghanistan: It was easier on the bones than that greater-DC-area swamp. My broken body felt better than it had since I'd strode into South Africa more or less intact and exited limping.

I pulled my phone off my bedside table without getting up. Ten am? I'd taken one or three oxy too many last night, and really slept like a teenager.

It felt good, though. I felt good. Home. A home where I'd contributed to the slaughter of many innocents, and where a guy tried to kill me. Which, now that I thought about it, also described my original home, the United States of America, by now, too.

Everybody makes mistakes. One thing I'd learned is that the more painkillers you were on, the less self conscious you were about how much you'd ruined your own life and the lives of the people around you. Getting blown up had brought me that beautiful working knowledge.

And it had brought me Kwa Lele.

And Kwa Lele had sent me back here.

My phone rang.

Probably, to die.

I answered it, or at least, I tried. Hit the button over and over. Nothing happened.

Because it wasn't my cell phone ringing. It was my landline in my room.

When's the last time you heard one of those go off?

I rolled out of bed, and picked it up in the middle of its jarring jangle.

"Hello?"

"Mr. Schneider?"

"Yes."

"Note for you at SDA-1, in the NOX-side security station."

"Oh, okay. Thanks. Who left it?"

"I don't know, sir."

"Alright. Thanks."

I hung up.

I EDGED into the market slowly, carefully.

Another life lesson I wanted to learn if the masses in my body or the explosives outside my body didn't kill me within the next day, or week, or month: you don't have to do every single little thing that a note tells you to do.

You really *don't*.

I casually picked up a miniscule carved bust of Alexander the Great. He probably died here in Afghanistan, too.

"Sir, for you, good price on the Great head. You want to see some carpets?"

"I can see them from here."

The collective work of dozens of women and children skilled and painstaking hand labor was spread out behind him, stunning colors and shapes that burst behind his head.

I felt my own head was about to burst. Was there a laser sight on it? I wasn't worth a laser sight. I wasn't El Chapo or The Jackal. Somebody could have easily taken me down with a well-placed rock throw.

"I make you an offer," he said. And he slipped a piece of paper into my hand before I even saw his move.

Then he turned his back on me.

Another note.

I took his cue and walked away from him, covert as elephants covered in lube tiptoeing through a chime store. I did my best, though, my very best, to unfurl a tiny piece of paper and read it unnoticed, unsuspicious.

WALK AHEAD TURN THE CORNER RIGHT

THIS WAS IT, I was going to take the orders that shot me in the face, because I had no other ideas on what to do.

I walked the ten paces or so, putting one foot in front of the other, my heart pounding in my chest. A man swerved towards me. I gasped. He withdrew a cigarette from his pocket, kept on going, totally disinterested. I eyed every face in the bazaar, and then I hit the alley.

I waited for my head to explode.

Nothing.

I looked left. Mostly vacant. A couple of burqas. Either one could be my killer. I scanned the rooftops. My breath came in short, ragged bursts. A light wind blew dust into my eyes. I squinted and rubbed them free.

By the time I opened them again, I was still alive.

On the right, one car parked in the alley. A dusty old Toyota, missing its left headlight.

The right headlight flashed twice.

A hand waved.

Rahim.

I shuffled over and practically dove into the car.

I was so relieved to see him.

By the look on his face, it wasn't mutual.

"Get in. Fast. Fast. Get in."

"I *am* in! I thought you were going to kill me."

"If I did, I would get a lot of money."

"What?"

"There's a reward for killing you." Rahim tugged on his beard like he always did in times of trouble: the moment I'd discovered the debacle at site B, the day the delegation had come to site A, anytime Artie farted openly in our miniscule trailer.

"A reward? From who?"

"Mr. Jim, the cartel is after you."

"Rahim—why aren't you driving?"

"You look terrible. May Allah have mercy."

"I got blown up. I'm addicted to painkillers. Things haven't been great. Let's go, drive. The cartel. Who are they?" Rahim tore his eyes away from what was apparently a hideous rendition of myself that I was presenting, started the car, and backed out of the alley.

"The cartel is more active than ever. They extracted Site A."

"All of it?"

"All. Now they're going after B, and we have to stop them."

I couldn't stop anything if my life depended on it.

A guy drifted by on a bike, lazily, I thought, and a little unsteady. He swerved at Rahim's side.

"Allah," Rahim said.

Before he finished the word, there was a click on the door.

"Go! GO GO GO," he shouted.

I froze. I heard my ragged breathing and my heart up in my mind. I couldn't move. My legs were stuck to the rusted floor of that Corolla.

Rahim lunged over me, elbowing me square in the gut. He unlatched the door, kicked it open, and shoved me out into the dirt with both hands.

He heaved himself out the same side, stumbled over me, and dragged me up, running me down the alley, pushing me ahead of him.

Red hot flecks burned the back of my neck and I smelled my hair burning and I was tossed to the ground again, Rahim beside me.

Rahim belly crawled away a pace, then reached back and yanked me along.

"Crawl," He hissed. "There could be others." It broke my freeze, and I slithered and shimmied down the alley alongside Rahim until we were at the far end of the alley.

My wrecked arm and leg hurt and I felt a burn deep in my guts. Maybe shrapnel. We slunk and crawled the length of the alley down in the dust.

Finally Rahim stopped.

And I stopped.

Everybody was a potential combatant. My chest was heaving. A little boy ran up to us and I flinched. He pointed at Rahim's burning car and said something to him I didn't understand. Rahim turned to me.

"Let's go," he said.

"What?" I shouted. "Go where?"

"It's not safe out here."

"Inside a stranger's house?"

"He's not a stranger. He's my nephew."

Do you usually invite your child relatives to your own bombing? I didn't say that. It was inflammatory and not at all the truth. Was it?

Rahim came here to help me, to save my life. I could trust him, he was one of the few people who regularly occurred in my life who I could trust. Inviting suspicion into that would kill me for sure.

We picked ourselves up and dusted ourselves off. Rahim was moving okay for a guy who had just been in an explosion, but I was torn up from the whole series. My ankle screamed every time I walked on it, and so did I, I hop-limp-screamed after them, inviting terrorists to trail and kill us.

Rahim's nephew led us to the right, down that silt-dirt road, surrounded on both sides by a kariz run dry. Full sun. If our killers were after us, they could have seen us from a mile away. Or a kilometer.

Kilometers overseas. Miles in America.

I wasn't focusing right. Mentally or visually. Probably shock. Again.

We wound through a little enclave of houses, passed a well and another crumbling wall. A stray dog trotted by us on some business in the opposite direction, tits swinging, not interested in us. A few men squatted on the low wall, stopped their conversation when we passed. Rahim said something to them. One of them eyed me and it didn't look favorable.

"Rahim, maybe we shouldn't..."

"We have nowhere else to go. My car is blown up. The only way out is through."

Through what? I wanted to say. I didn't know if he'd given up trying to explain something or if he was being metaphorical. Hadn't somebody else said that to me recently? The only way *out* is *through*. What a dumb catchphrase. This was just like failing forward. What would they come up with next? Dying up?

Rahim led me into the courtyard, flanked by four adjoined buildings, snaked me into its center. A whole crowd waiting for us. The Afghan youths. I wouldn't have recognized them, except I saw the three up front, the ones I knew best: Cigarette Smoker, Afghan Elvis, and Unwestern Clothes.

Afghan Elvis nodded and waved to us.

"What is this, Rahim?"

"Assembly," he said.

Guns everywhere. Ancient-looking crates along the side with unreadable Russian words on them. You could imagine, though, because the boxes were full of—

"Kalashnikovs," Rahim said, nodding.

"Rahim. These kids *are* terrorists."

"Not terrorists," Rahim said."*Counter* terrorists. This is a big difference. The *real* terror is the country of Sweden."

Who the hell was going to believe that? He waved Afghan Elvis over, said a word to the boy, and then took a spot at the front of the room.

"I'm Daud," he said. "Do you remember me?"

I nodded.

"I'm going to translate for you," Daud said. "What Rahim says. And here's some bandage for you." He handed me a strip of cloth.

"Okay," I said. "Thank you." My pants were torn at the bottom left cuff, and a couple of good-sized patches of skin were gone off my shin and ankle, both shallow, and I'd clotted by now. I tied the cloth around my leg wound anyway, to be polite.

No sign of running water. Or hydrogen peroxide. Or Neosporin. Or anything else that used to be my protocol for a cut that was over a quarter of an inch. Maybe a really active, angry bacteria would shake up my body's immune system, remind it to fight whatever the masses near my heart and stomach were.

Rahim pulled a Kalashnikov out of the crate and banged it on the table at the front of the room, three times to get the room's attention. And he spoke.

"My dear sirs," Daud translated. "Thank you for coming here today."

I noticed for the first time that it wasn't exclusively young people. There was a mix of ages in the room, a few elderly, even.

"For generations, we waited. And watched. We knew this time would come, the prophecy has been fulfilled."

"My father told it to me. Just as your fathers told it to you. His father told it to him."

"The time has come for retaliation."

Rahim opened all the crates that lined the walls, one per sentence.

"The imposter will say to you, I am the word."

An elderly man lifted a Kalashnikov out of the crate and echoed Rahim's last phrase.

"I am the word," the room repeated in unison.

"The imposter will say to you, I am the light," Daud said.

Rahim handed a gun to the closest, who echoed him.

"When Sirius C becomes visible in the sky—" Daud said.

What?

"The earth's electromagnetic field will weaken—"

"They will use the blood to activate the serpents—"

"Wait, what?" I said to Daud. He ignored me.

"And ascend from this world to claim their destiny—"

"And destroy everything else in the process unless you stop it."

"And they will all say to you:"

"I am the light. And the life—"

"And the one true way."

"But you will know they are lying."

"They have the heads of serpents, and you must act fast."

"You must act fast, you must act fast," Daud said over and over again. The room joined Rahim, standing, chanting, and they hoisted their guns to the sky.

"INTERNATIONAL SOCIETY OF ROSICRUCIANS, AFGHANISTAN CHAPTER," Rahim said proudly. "I lead the resistance against Sweden."

"I thought that was for Christians," I said.

"It's not. It's for people who don't want to get murdered by Swedes. Muslims included."

Rahim pointed a long finger down into the mineshaft. We huddled around the rim of the wreckage of Site A.

"Do you see that rock, sticking up over there?"

"That rock? Ohhhh that rock. No, Rahim, it's all one big rock."

Rahim kept patient. He knew by now my white western spread-sheet-reading eyes were defective.

"Follow the vein down with your face, then to the right three degrees. You see?"

I did as I was told, and there, next to Mineral X's red iridescent glow, I saw it. There was something else. It looked like a blue-clad quicksilver, mercury. Same as the day before the delegation, I remembered suddenly.

I'd forgotten so much.

"I saw it," I said.

Or was it a silver green? It was changing before my eyes.

It *moved*.

Towards me.

I scrambled back from the mineshaft.

"Did you see that?"

"I've *been* seeing that," Rahim said. "For years."

"I saw it before, I'd forgotten. The day of the delegation. When Artie tried to blow me up. I didn't know what I was doing, it was like I blacked out. And I woke up touching it, and then I...heard you, and Artie, and other people inside my own head."

"Like a mineral corpus callosum that unites human minds," Rahim said.

"That's what all this is about?" I asked.

"That's what all this is about," he echoed. He gestured around at the burned-down trailer, the small fires of debris all around us. "Nobody else can be exposed to it and live. I should say, be allowed to live. By the Swedes. If too many people access it, it will ruin their plan."

"What's the plan?" I asked.

"I don't know," he said. "Something in the United States."

"But you knew already that it wasn't good to touch it," I said. "You *knew* and you pushed the inspections training anyway. Why?"

"We all knew, and we decided to do it. We made the decision together through the loya jirga twenty years ago. Our fathers told us what would happen if we didn't." Rahim pointed at the mud hut, I didn't know why. "Because there is no risk at all that we don't face anyway, if the Swedes take enough of it and get it out of here."

"What risk?"

This cold concrete sludge was running up my legs, both at once. I didn't know if it was my own fear or the thing from the mine, working on me.

"It's the mineral that ends the world," he said. "It's the death of all of us."

30

AFTER TWENTY MINUTES

After twenty minutes of *trying* to have sex with Diane, I started to wonder if Elise had killed herself to get away from me rather than from some toxic mesh cutting through her insides and poisoning her brain.

"No," Diane said. "Here." She moved my hands down until they gripped her ass instead of the small of her back.

Elise never gave this much direction or had this many complaints.

"Harder," Diane grunted.

I grinded my hips against hers and she rose up to meet them, sucking air between gasps. Sex was a lot of work at altitude, with my body torn up three times over now, and all hopped up on painkillers. I felt my already mediocre erection start to slip and go mushy.

I squeezed my eyes shut and pictured Kwa Lele, leaning in to listen to me in her prison cell. I parted Diane's government thighs.

Kwa Lele's eyes. Bright, burning.

I sucked on Diane's right breast, the one that had its eye on me, and used my thumb to skim the nipple on the one that looked to the left.

Her smooth skin.

Diane grabbed the fleshiest part of my ass, yanked me down, and wrapped her legs around me in return.

The scars, her legs.

Kwa Lele pulling me up out of the dirt, explosion debris floating around her head like a halo.

I hardened all the way, and I drove into Diane with everything I had.

The phone rang.

Diane startled a little, but enough that I could feel it, then pushed me off and ran towards the phone, drawing the sheet around to hide her body from me, even though my dick was just in her and I didn't think we had many secrets at this point.

"Hello? Oh," she said. "Mom. Hi."

Diane held up a finger.

"Mom, I don't know what the dosage is. I know I do, mom. Yes. It doesn't mean I know anything about them. I'm not a doctor. Billy's doctor will know. I think they've got a handle on what to do. God knows he's been there enough times."

She pointed at the phone and shrugged at me. My penis shriveled. This session was over, regardless of when the call ended.

"No, it never works. You're right," she said into the phone. She turned her back on me. Her dad had died of heroin. Now her brother was on his way, she'd said the week prior over gin and tonics at the Duck and Cover. Music blaring. Laser lights on the walls, spinning. Dance floor packed. She threw a dart at a dartboard after she'd said, 'On his way.'

She'd trounced me at darts. Most of mine didn't even wind up on the board. Drinking on pills made everything feel like it was happening in freshly poured concrete.

After more listening and stock responses, Diane came back to bed.

"I'm sorry," she said. "Where were we?"

But it was a token gesture, I could see, not a real effort to get restarted, which was totally out of the question for me anyway, so I pulled her close, settled her in on my fat stomach, pulled those sandpaper sheets around us and said nothing. Talking about her brother's rehab was neither lubricant nor Viagra. She curled her legs around mine and lay her head on my chest. Sex with me was so disappointing, I knew if women came back for more, it was because they were desperate for intimacy of any kind.

I stroked Diane's hair, which was a little better than I ever did for Elise. Kwa Lele, would she ever let me touch her? Never. She would never have me. Why did she save my life, twice? I considered the rational possibilities that existed, which were

1. to use me later
2. to frame me for Ravi's death
3. to use me as a pawn to get out of the clutches of the Russian-Swedish-Afghan-US mineral cartel or Pauly, or whatever the hell, God, who knew what, or
4. was she a part of the cartel herself?

I rose after this last, most unpalatable thought, and went to the sink to bring Diane some water.

"Oh, don't use that," Diane said, after I turned on the tap. "All these pipes are bad. There was an OIG report. Came out a couple of months ago. "

"All of them? The whole compound?"

"Yep. Whole thing. Nothing is up to code."

"What? I drank this water for months before I left for South Africa."

"Yeah, even with daily view of the goddamned site, every minute of every day, full access, we still can't get anything built to specs around here. Imagine what's going on out there." Diane pointed out at Afghanistan, the thousands of miles that no US government worker ever set foot on unless armed to the teeth. "There's bottled water in the fridge."

I fished one out and brought it over to her, climbed back into bed. Her apartment might have had poisonous water, but so did my CHU, and at least her apartment had more than a twin-sized bed in it. I wasn't in a hurry to leave.

"Do you think it's safe in here? To talk?"

"Sure," she said. "What, do you think you're tapped?"

I eyed Diane. Polly and Paul were in bed with the Russians. We also had Swedes, Americans, Afghans. Who was Diane in bed with?

Besides me? At the moment.

"I guess no more than the next government employee. I don't understand, why would our *own* government try to undermine confidence in our *own* mineral extraction project?"

"It's easier to mishandle extraction of precious minerals in a corrupt administration than not," Diane said. "Plus it's not even our real government. It's a foreign government hidden inside our government."

"That's too many governments," I said. "I used to believe in government conspiracies," I said. "But that was before I started working for the government. Nobody has that kind of organizational skill. Do they?"

"What if you made the richest countries in the world fat, and then sold the cure for their fatness back to them? Great business model, isn't it?"

"Crazy," I said. But did she know about the thing *next* to Mineral X? If she did, she wasn't spilling the beans on that one.

"Crazy," Diane said. "Sure. Plus, overwhelmingly profitable. Destabilizing. And, unlike a nuclear attack, largely untraceable to its source."

Diane patted my head the same way I'd patted the head of our second dog moments before we had to put him down.

"Why are you telling me all this?"

"You're a good guy. I could tell the first day I saw you. And you're in way over your head."

"What gave it away, the way I swooned in the heat and altitude? Or getting blown up three times since you've known me?"

Diane grinned, and cupped my balls. "Woman's intuition," she said. "I'm glad you're back."

"What are *you* going to do, Diane?" Rob the mine again?

"The same thing any government worker does. Keep my head down and do what I'm told. If it were one person, or one political party, or one drug company that was responsible for this, I suppose I might whistleblow. Call in an anonymous tip. But it's across the board. Both sides. All sides. I'm talking about a foreign presence so immersed in our own, I don't even know who I *could* tell."

"What do you think would happen? Would they kill you?"

"I used to think that would be far-fetched."

"Before Ravi?"

"Yes, before Ravi. Now I know they have total impunity."

"Or they think they do."

Diane rose from the bed. "You'd better go," she said. "I'm meeting some friends for lunch."

"Guess I'll just walk-of-shame back to my CHU."

Part of me wanted an invite to lunch, and the other part was glad to be dismissed, get the hell out of there. I got up and stepped into my pants on the floor, struggled them up and sucked in my gut before I could even think about zippering.

"Can I stop by later? I have some documents of Ravi's that I want you to take a look at. From his wife."

"Sure," Diane shrugged. "I'll be back around 8 or so."

"Okay. Thanks. Thanks for everything, Diane."

Her face was unreadable, and she turned away from me quickly to grab her robe.

"No problem, Jim."

No kiss goodbye.

DIANE DIDN'T RETURN any of my text messages. I lurked in the lobby of her building at 6 pm, and after dinner I drifted over again at 8 pm. Finally, when she didn't turn up by 11 pm, I gave up. It would have to wait until tomorrow.

The next day, Diane was nowhere to be found. All my calls went to voicemail. I went to the front desk.

"I'm looking for Diane Rodinger," I said to the Gurkha at the front desk. He pulled out a worn binder and flipped through the pages. I wanted to make polite small talk based on the last time I had seen him, but I couldn't tell if he was the same guy or not.

"Diane, Diane," he said. "Not here."

"What? What do you mean, 'not here'? I saw her last week. Did you look under Rodinger?"

"Maybe she moved. Didn't tell you." He didn't smile.

"You know what?" I said. "You're right. I forgot that she was going to move. I was in there yesterday, though, for a little going-away party, and I left my meal card up there. Do you think you could let me in, real quick?"

I didn't know what the hell I thought I was doing.The first step towards a successful investigation is getting into places they're trying to keep you out of, right? Maybe that was the oxy talking.

"Okay," he said. "No problem." He said a few things into his walkie talkie and after a few minutes another security Gurkha showed up. Then he grabbed a ring of keys and led me to the elevator.

Success. I had lied my way into Diane's apartment.

It was, indeed, completely empty.

As if Diane didn't exist at all.

My heart started working harder, thudding in a more painful way.

"It should be over by the bed," I said to him.

"Sure," he said. "No problem."

But there *were* problems. Lots of them.

I entered the bedroom and opened every drawer in the dresser, nothing. I looked under the bed. What the hell did I expect to find under the dumb bed? Some evidence that Diane existed. And then, when en route to the kitchen, when I headed over to root around in the trash, there, on the side of the refrigerator, I did see some evidence that Diane existed. Diane, and another woman.

Another woman.

On a cruise.

Who I knew.

There was Diane.

There was Diane's arm.

There were the shoulders of Jane Foxhall.

My heart pounded harder. Then it did a little flip inside my chest, expanded into a squeezing ache that closed my throat. I couldn't breathe.

"Sir?" The Gurke stepped over the threshold. "Sir, are you okay?"

I wasn't. My vision tunneled. I clutched the sides of the garbage can. I felt myself start to slip, and then I blacked out.

I OPENED my eyes to the institutionally-tiled ceiling of the base infirmary. Since I had taken this job, I had woken up in hospitals following an unintentional loss of consciousness one hundred percent of the time. Bad stats. Or good ones, depending on your goals and your views on healthcare.

"Hey, there you are! We thought we were going to have to Medivac you out of here."

"Paul?" I hadn't seen him yet since I'd returned.

"Good. You're remembering names. That's a great sign."

"Did I have a stroke?"

"No, sir." He chuckled. "Panic attack is more like it."

"I was looking for Diane. Where is she?"

"DEA transferred her. Last minute change. Nothing to worry about. I'm sure she'll email you soon. Did we kindle a little compound romance?"

I winced. "No."

"Hard on the heart," Paul said.

"Just a friendship."

"Good," Paul said. "It can get lonely here on the base. Nothing to do but exercise and think. It's nice to have a friend." He winked. I winced.

You raped a child, you son of a bitch. You raped a child and now you've murdered Diane, and I'm going to find a way to kill you.

My phone buzzed, inside my pants, slung over the visitor's chair.

"Could you hand me that phone?" I asked.

"Sure," he said. And he did.

It said:

SITE A

31

SITE A WAS

S ite A was completely razed, unrecognizable from its former self. I only knew roughly where things used to be because the burned-up husks of them still stood: shell of the FDA trailer, frame of the MRI trailer.

Bombed again, since Rahim and I had visited. They must have put it on a regular schedule. No skin off anybody's back to send a drone out a few times a day.

The railing was still there, attached to a disembodied chunk of concrete.

And next to it, a pile of laundry.

Or a person.

"Yes, here is fine," I said to the taxi driver. I paid him and he didn't question me.

"Tashakor," he said. If he didn't speak English, there was no way for him to.

"Tashakor," I said, and I made my way down to the pile of laundry.

"Jim, it's me," the bundle of robes hissed.

"Ravi?"

He edged closer. I could make out a Ravi-sized shape under all that linen now.

"What the hell are you doing here? What the hell are you doing...alive?"

"Man, I had to fake my own death."

"Give me a second." I was panting hard, dizzy. "I gotta stop taking these pills."

"What do they have you on?"

"Oxy."

"Oh, that's rough. Are you addicted yet? Maybe you can get in on the class action."

"There's a class action?"

"Several."

I exhaled and gripped the railing, the only thing that was recognizable of our old site. Everything else had been stripped, ripped, or otherwise shredded, burned.

"What do we do?"

"I dunno, man. I'm mixed up in some serious shit and I don't know how to get out of it."

"So you faked your own death."

A molten draft blew up from the collapsed mineshaft and ruffled Ravi's cloaks around him.

"They were going to hurt Priya and the kids. I didn't have a choice."

"What are you going to do now?"

"I don't know, Jim. I really don't. If Rahim hadn't found a place for me to land I don't know what I would be doing now. Bin Laden hid out in the caves here for decades, didn't he?"

"I guess. I think he had millions of dollars, an extensive network of supporters, and he was, I don't know, more resilient?"

"Yeah. I don't know how I'm going to make it. I really don't. I miss Priya. I miss the kids. I can't believe I'm putting her through this."

"Who, exactly, is going to kill you though?"

"I don't know, Jim! They don't, like, invite me out to a Starbucks and show me their IDs. I thought it was the CIA. Then it turned out to be this group of Senators, Fletch Senior, all his cronies. Then I started thinking, maybe it's not the United States Government. Hell, I don't know."

"Kwa Lele told me she gutted you like a fish."

"She saved my life," Ravi said. "They were gonna kill me. Hack off my arms or legs or something. Awful."

"Why?"

"Because of my haplogroup," he said.

"Your what?"

"My haplogroup. I have a genetic material they need. And so does she. They're not only hunting this obesity drug, Jim. They're hunting certain types of people, too. And then, it's not the obesity drug after all. It's another thing. That grows next to Mineral X. That's what they're really after. What they've really been after all along. And if you get exposed to it..."

"Yeah, I know. Who do you think *they* are?" I asked.

"Swedes," he said. "I know it sounds crazy, but they're Swedes."

"Swedes," I said.

"People from Sweden," he said. So there could be no mistake.

But Jane Foxhall wasn't a Swede. Nor was Diane. Or Paul. Or Polly. And they were all implicated somehow, too.

"Swedes," I said again. I really couldn't get past it. And if we hadn't had at least one in the delegation at Site A, I wouldn't have believed it, either.

"They really stripped this place, huh?"

Site A was a scorched earth campaign married to the lousiest terrace job.

"You should see Site B," he said. "They brought in the biggest strip miner they could find. They're getting ready to do the same. Or they were before I got jettisoned."

"They haven't done it yet. Rahim's leading an insurrection."

"You don't say."

"Against the Swedes. He says if they can overtake Site B before they get enough of the mineral out, it'll ruin their plan."

"Maybe," Ravi said. "I don't even know what their plan is."

"Have you touched it? The mineral?"

"I did a little worse than that, Jim. I injected it."

"You *injected* it?"

"Many, many, many times. And now I can't be more than a few kilometers from the largest deposits in the world. Which are right here. Looks like I'm a resident of Afghanistan now. For life. Or until...we figure something else out."

"Who's we?"

"Me and Jane Foxhall."

"She in on this?" If she was, then Diane was. Diane hadn't levelled with me about the thing next to Mineral X. Maybe she was protecting me. Or maybe she was setting me up.

Either way, now she was missing.

"She is. One of the good guys."

"Are you sure?"

"I am, yeah. She saved my life."

I wasn't sure if there were any good guys yet.

"What's with your rags?"

"Trying to stay out of drone sight," Ravi said. "They're everywhere, Eagle Eye-style. I wish there was a way to destroy this thing."

"Isn't there? Maybe that's our ticket out?"

"I don't think so. I don't think it catches on fire."

"What about if you nuke it?"

"I don't know."

"Doesn't that destroy, like, everything?"

"I don't know, man. I'm a geneticist, not a nuclear engineer. I'm way out of my league on all this, that's been the problem the whole time. I don't know *who* I'm working for, I don't know who *they're* working for, I don't know what *we're* doing, and I don't know *why* we're doing it. I've just been trying to survive. They threatened to kill my wife and kids."

"God, almighty," I said, with disgust, my voice a séanced version of my dead dad.

Ravi and I brainstorming wasn't going to lead to anything. We were real bureaucrats. Taking orders, collecting our paycheck, solution-free, good at staring at a simple spreadsheet, injecting some rats, then ourselves, with a goo. And that was about it.

"Everything's riding on Rahim," Ravi said. "Maybe the insurrection will save us all."

"Do you think so?"

"No. But it's worth a try. What else do we have to lose?" Ravi shook his head. He uprighted the downed dirt bike next to him, shuffled his rags around so he could seat himself, kicked it into action and chugged away.

I watched him disappear over the stripped horizon.

32

RAHIM AND I

Rahim and I had been running pre-insurrection errands all day. I was exhausted, head on the headrest, tired of jouncing up and down, all my injuries really making themselves known.

And then a shiny Suburban in our rearview caught my eye. Caught it and held it, with its aggressive driving.

"I think we're being followed, Rahim."

The Suburban overtook us, cut off Rahim's replacement Corolla, only slightly more rusted than the blown up Corolla.

"Not anymore," he said.

"Pull up to them! Embassy plates. It's Polly and Paul, it's got to be."

"If you know who it is, why do I have to do a chase?"

That was a good point.

"I need to be sure." That wasn't true. Why was I initiating car chases all of a sudden? Must have been the oxy talking.

Rahim banked the Toyota hard, pulled over to the side, stopped short of putting us into the kariz. The Suburban breezed through the intersection, weaving between an overwhelming volume of cars and people packed into an impossibly small area of pavement, and they hit the circle at high speed. Rahim pulled up short to avoid knocking over a kid tugging his shoe repair cart behind him that had ambled out into the road.

"Rahim, what the hell are you doing? They're getting away!"

Rahim took time away from letting the enemy escape to give me a shut-up-look.

"I know where they're going," he said. "They won't get away."

"You do? How?"

"Because they just texted me," he said. He held up his phone.

SITE A

TWENTY MINUTES LATER, we were at Site A. The Suburban was waiting.

I got out. Rahim got out.

Four men with guns got out.

And Diane.

"You," I said. "I thought they'd murdered you."

"I'm in the DEA, Jim."

"Yeah, I know."

"Who's going to murder me?"

"I don't know, Diane. Why don't you tell me?"

"You've got to back off on all this, Jim."

"I know," I said. It threw her off, wasn't what she was expecting.

"It's bigger than Mineral X, Jim."

"I know," I said again.

Diane mumbled something out of my earshot to either her four armed captors or protectors, I still didn't know which one they were. The one closest to me looked like an orc extra off Lord of the Shittier-Quality Rings, Kabul edition.

Somebody else was still in the car.

I couldn't help but feel things would have gone better between me and Diane if I hadn't done such a bad job of eating her pussy.

Instead, I said:

"Give Jane Foxhall my regards," with a sneer.

"Jim, I wasn't keeping that from you. It just didn't come up."

"What's your angle, Diane?"

"It's not personal, I'll tell you that."

"I hear you. I do. But we did have sex, multiple times, so it is a little bit personal, Diane. It is personal when you disappear, and you don't tell the person you slept with earlier that day."

Diane winced. "Yes, that does sound personal, when you say it like that," she said.

She had a gun.

"And that's kinda personal, too," I said, nodding at the gun.

I hadn't registered it right away. Ravi thought Jane Foxhall was a good guy. I wasn't convinced. And I had no idea, anymore, about Diane. This evidence seemed to be to the contrary. She trained the gun on me and then Rahim. Tiny little gun. Her eyes looked a twinge gleeful. Maybe she was going to *enjoy* killing us. Shooting a guy who did a bad job eating her out and also some other guy next to him.

"Rahim, get back in the car," I said to him.

"I'm scared to move," he said, and he didn't.

"So you're joining them?" I said to Diane. "Deciding on treason?"

"Not treason, Jim. Jane and I tried to fight this. We did. For a decade. More. But I'm tired. I'm really tired, Jim. Tired of fighting. They offered money, so I took it. I'm not a bad person. Money, and a way out. My mom's dying. My brother's an addict. I want to go home. That's all I want now."

"Who did, Diane? Who offered you money?"

"The Swedes," Diane said. "Lanna Bergström." Diane said *Lanna Bergström* the way you would say *chronic toenail fungus*.

"She gotcha, huh? Her and that incredible neck."

"That neck and ten million. Not even enough to live on, just to settle up for all my troubles."

The car door opened. Again, neither Paul nor Polly. Every single one of my theories about who was doing what for whom and what had caused anything to happen in this whole miserable mess had been dead wrong.

It was Artie.

"I didn't know you two were friends," I said.

"I had one job to do here, you *idiot*," Artie said. "One fucking thing I wanted to achieve: keep everybody away from that poisonous shit next to Mineral X until the Swedes could yank it out the ground and sneak it out the back door. And what did you do? You invited every single asshole in a ten mile radius to come touch it. They're all dead, Jim."

My body ran cold, slurry in my veins.

"No," I said.

"I don't have any children of my own, me and the missus. Not a one. She's barren. I shoot blanks. No chance in hell of reproducing. When I got here, I said to myself, you know what, Artie, you old coot, *these* are your children." He lost control, banged the roof of the Suburban, five times in rapid succession. Got himself back together. Leaned against the side of the car like he'd been pulled over by the cops. "Every young person in a 100 mile-radius around your mines, *they* can be your kids. And as their dad, your job, *my* job, my *only* job, was to keep them the fuck away from Mineral X, and that poisonous shit next to it."

"The Swedes are gonna kill them all, Jim," Diane said.

"And then you showed up," Artie spit.

Diane shook her head.

"Can't have them touching the goods, Jim. It destroys the purity. The Swedes are gonna have to drag every single one of those Afghan kids out of their homes and shoot them in the head."

"You murdered them," Artie said. "All my adopted Afghan kids."

Artie was the good guy here, not me.

"Dead because of you."

He was the one who was keeping everybody safe. By keeping them away.

Maybe I *should* get a bullet in my head. Not Rahim, though.

"I didn't know," I said. "I didn't know the obesity shit was a cover. Mineral X."

"It's not a cover," Diane said. "That's all real, too."

"But it's not the star of the show, Jim." Artie nodded at Diane, both of them older and sadder in the face than when we first met. Was that the go-ahead to kill us?

"I didn't know when I set up the inspections program, and I didn't know when—"

I side-eyed Rahim, willing him to psychically give me the go-ahead to divulge everything, to buy us another day of life. His face was unreadable. I had to make this decision on my own.

"—when we organized an insurrection, either."

Diane sighed, threw her head back to address the sky with her eyes. Got this fly-in-my-coffee look of disgust on, and pointed it at me. Pointed that gun at me again, too.

She might pull the trigger due to intense irritation.

"But we did," I said. "We did. And it's gonna be a mess if you don't let us live long enough to call it off."

Artie got back in the car, slammed the door. After a long pause, Diane did too. And they drove off.

"Well, that was easy," I said.

"Easy, peasy," Rahim agreed.

"What's next?" I said. "Anything else we need to do before we blast Site B?"

Rahim reached into the backseat and grabbed a small sack, pulled an elastic band out of it. Rolled up my sleeve and tied the band around my flabby bicep.

"Rahim, what's that?"

He tapped my vein, tap tap tap.

"Rahim? What are you doing?"

"This is necessary," he said.

"What is?"

He pulled a needle out of the bag, a loaded hypodermic, jabbed it into my arm, and pressed go on whatever the hell the contents were before I could yank away. Which I did, needle in. I tore the needle out. But whatever had been in *it* was already in *me*.

I took a deep breath, filled my lungs all the way up to scream my protest.

By the time I could make any sound, Rahim's mind was my own.

Alhamdulillah, I exhaled.
The mineral corpus callosum of all humans, Rahim thought.

And in so thinking, so did I.
زما تليفون زما په جيب کې بوج
شو

My phone buzzed in my pocket.

WE PULLED it out and arrowed into the message.

My wife.
An emergency.
The kids.
We had to go there.
Now.

33

THE CHILDREN ARE

ماشومان ورک شوي

"The children are gone!"

Anar screamed, knelt down in the dirt behind the house. Our kitchen window broken through, glass in the sink, yard door shattered.

Scrap of paper on the interior, wrapped around a brick on the floor and one in the sink.

"God will protect them," I said, and I knew He would. "God is closer to them than the jugular veins in their throats."

ANAR CONTINUED to scream until she blacked out, and it reminded me of losing my own children.

On the scrap of paper, it said,

موږ ته بيروکريټ راکړئ يا

ماشومان به مړه شي

Give us the bureaucrat, or the children will die.

"NOT A PROBLEM," I said. "Happy to do it. I just have one errand left."

34

RAHIM PULLED UP

Rahim pulled up to the compound.

"I'm sorry," he said. "It was the only way. The more minds we add, the better chance we have at success. But it was not supposed to happen like this."

No, of course not. Kids aren't supposed to be kidnapped or killed. Especially not in the middle of the first time you network your brain to that of an unwilling colleague without any advance warning or prep, because there just isn't enough time for that bullshit.

"No problem," I said. "See you tomorrow?" I elbowed the glove compartment, "You'll drop it for me?"

He nodded. Good guy. The kind who would hide a glock in the bushes outside L'Atmosphere for you. I'd show up tomorrow and get traded to some Swedish terrorists for Rahim's kids: one for two.

When he pulled away, my brain got a lot clearer, more detached from his. I stopped hearing his thoughts. It also got a lot foggier. My pain was back, and along with it, my burning desire to swallow a fistful of oxycodone.

I no longer understood Dari, Pashto, or any other language besides English. That junk next to Mineral X was a hell of a drug, for sure, but it didn't work at a distance.

I still had this residual feeling inside that unsettled me, a driving impulse compelling me to act. And when I dug deep on what it was, I realized it was Rahim's faith, lingering in my brain. Not a typical part of me or of my personality, my usual line of thinking.

Paul agreed to meet for dinner that night.

He didn't even ask what it was about.

AFTER DINNER and dessert and drinks at L'Atmosphere, I said to Paul, "How about a little walk?"

"Sure," he said. "If the operative word in this sentence is *little*."

We both chuckled.

We'd eaten duck paté on Melba toasts, a dinner roll with one pat of butter, each, two-plus glasses of Merlot, split-the-bottle-style, with equality of access and consumption. Paul hadn't gotten enough duck with just the liver mashup, so he went on to have the roast duck and frites.

Frites. That was French for French fries, it turned out.

He dipped them in mayonnaise, which was a revelation to me.

I tried the chicken parmesan. It was no Olive Garden, but it wasn't bad. For dessert he had the chocolate mousse, and I had the cheesecake. After, we had an aperitif, and then a fine scotch about which I knew nothing. Paul was well-versed.

He was still nursing his scotch.

I was ready to go.

"Listen," I said. "I appreciate everything you've done for me."

"Don't mention it," he said. And he didn't register that he hadn't done anything for me.

He talked for another twenty minutes about his lengthy career trying to help the poor and unfortunate refugees of this earth get back on their feet, a gargantuan task, a massive challenge that he found himself continuously rising to meet.

"How about that walk?" I said again.

This was the most challenging part of the whole endeavor. Getting Paul to agree to a walk.

"One of the things about temporary housing structures," Paul said. "Is, there's a lot of money to be made in it."

He wouldn't do it, walk.

"Oh, is there?" I drained my scotch. It burned all the way down. I wasn't much of a drinker.

"So you get all these hangers-on, contractors playing around the fringe. I saw it all. Twenty years with UNHCR. Like, failed styrofoam dealers who try to pretend to you that it's a house."

"Do they?" I said. I raised my finger. One more, I mouthed. I pointed to my glass. "Twenty years," I said.

I was going to get drunk, and then I was going to shoot this son of a bitch right in his mouth.

"I briefly met Sérgio Vieira de Mello before we lost him in Iraq," he said.

"Oh, really?" I said.

If I could ever get him outside.

"I KNOW WHAT YOU DID. I know what you did to her, you son of a bitch." I mumbled, one hand on the wall, one hand on my junk, pissing into the urinal.

Kwa Lele's face, that night she told me what Paul did.

Paul. Head of Refugees and Migration.

I don't know what came over me, maybe it *was* my mind, breaking. Maybe I couldn't stand one more wrong nobody even tried to right. I know I'm not a hero. I don't have any authority to dispense justice. But I was going to anyway.

I waited for the automatic soap dispenser to do its thing, studied myself in the mirror. I looked like absolute hell. I'd finally inherited my dad's eye bags.

I couldn't help but wonder if it was faith. Religious fanatics were right after all. All things are possible. With faith.

I rejoined the table.

"About ready?" Paul asked. He'd been gracious enough to let me pay the bill, to throw down my credit card before I went to take a leak. It was more than Rahim made in two months' work, I noticed. I added the tip and signed off on it.

"Please," I said. "Let's."

"Have you phoned the car?" He asked. He hefted himself up out of the chair. No totter, no wobble in him. He could hold his alcohol. Unlike me.

"I have," I lied.

The security guards checked us out, but we didn't have any firearms to collect from the lockers. You could roll around anywhere you wanted with an AK-47 slung over your shoulder in Afghanistan, but they wouldn't let you bring it to dinner.

We waited out by the fountain in L'Atmosphere's roundabout.

"I thought you called the car," Paul said. "Risky to be out here all by ourselves."

There was a distant dog bark over and over again, but otherwise the night was quiet. The neighborhood was sparse over by L'Atmosphere.

"I did," I said. "I'll check on them." I walked a few paces up, took my phone out of my pocket. Counted the rosebushes. One. Two. Three. Four.

Stomach-sized mass behind the fourth rosebush, wrapped in a rag. I pulled the gun out and slipped it into my pocket, put my eyes on Paul. He was dicking around with his phone, looking anxiously up the street in the opposite direction.

I walked back.

"Any luck?" He asked.

"I know what you did," I said.

"What?"

"I said, I know what you did."

"Jim, I didn't do anything to Diane. Why didn't you say something earlier? She got transferred, that's all. You're tired, you're not thinking clearly. Six months in Afghanistan will do that to anybody." Paul took a step forward. Like he thought he was the one with the gun. The sweat dripped off his temple.

"Not Diane, you pedophile. I saw that bitch yesterday. You *know* who I'm talking about."

His eyes widened a little.

Remembering when he raped a kid over and over.

I pulled the gun out of my pocket.

"What are you doing?"

"You know what I'm doing," I said.

While my mind was thinking over and over again about what to do, my body pulled that trigger. It's so easy. I understood murderers for the first time in my life.

I didn't even wait to see what happened. I threw the gun into the bushes and I bolted, out and down the street.

I jogged through the darkened streets of Kabul, drunk, adrenaline shooting through my body, on the lookout for a taxi. My phone buzzed in my pocket. I fished it out.

MEET ME AT THE DFAC

YEAH, why not? I'd just murdered a man, so why not go for an anonymous meetup and a snack?

35

I HEARD THE

"I heard the broccoli is synthetic."

"What?" I said. The broccoli was greener than seemed possible, but it was a starker landscape around these parts. Maybe I had forgotten the color green, what it involved. Succulent little trees. I stood with my tray out and my plates all lined up, ready to shove some DFAC food in my mouth, no feelings about what I'd just done.

There was no way to tell Kwa Lele about it. That was the worst part.

It would be nice if, when somebody really evil who committed a vile act against you died, you felt it in your heart. That the harmed part of you got free, somehow. Not true at all, I was sad to admit to myself. She had no idea.

"It's synthetic. Part of some contract food experiment. That's what I heard. Have you tried it?"

"I haven't," I said.

"I just got here," the young woman turned from the steaming stainless steel buckets of food to appraise me fully. I hoped I didn't have blood on my shirt or alcohol on my breath. "Name's Jennifer Garner."

I looked down, did a quick spattered-blood-check. I was clean, in the clear. "Like the actress?" I asked. That was the wrong thing to say. Nobodies hated to be associated with their famous people names most of the time. You weren't supposed to meet somebody named John Wayne and start in with a *Howdy, Partner.*

"Yes," Jennifer Garner said. "Like the actress."

"Steer clear of the fake broccoli, Jennifer Garner. I recommend the Gurkha stuff off to the side." I nodded towards it. "Always a culinary pleasure."

"May I join you?" She asked.

"I'm afraid not," I said. "I'm meeting somebody already. Somebody awful. And I wouldn't want to put you through that."

"Oh," she said. "Thanks for sparing me."

"You're welcome," I said. "Anytime."

I slopped a few scoops of chicken curry onto my plates, nabbed an Arabic cola, and scanned the room until my eyes set on her.

"Hello, Polly," I said.

"Hello, Jim."

"What's the latest news?" I asked. I shoved a fork of chicken in my mouth, even less hungry than I was during the first dinner.

"They caught your girlfriend."

I choked until I had to spit my chicken out.

Polly said, "Take it easy. You smell drunk."

I killed your boyfriend. I didn't say it out loud.

Polly leaned in close. "This isn't some mamby-pamby minimum security jail with conjugal visits, Jim," she rasped, low in the busy dining hall. "They're gonna hang the bitch."

I wanted to put my fist right through Polly's face. I had never punched a human in my life. My fists and my guts were twitching like they wanted to throw down and throw up.

"How do we stop it?"

"I'll tell you how *we* stop it. *You* call off this stupid, childish little mutiny. Honestly, you have no idea what you're doing or who you're dealing with. Standing down is *our* first order of business."

"And you'll have her released?"

"Oh, Jim. I don't have that much power. You're really overestimating me. I'll put in a request for them to consider it."

"How do I know?"

"I'll CC you on the email."

They were emailing back and forth about her like Kwa Lele was some shipment of Tramadol that got lost in Customs. I was so mad I blacked out.

"I see what you're thinking," Polly said.

Did she?

"You want a piece of the action. I'll tell you what. You call off this little mutiny, I'll save your little girlfriend, and we'll even cut you in as a show of good faith."

Faith.

My brain slowly plodded through these words.

"Why'd you need us, Polly? We're nobodies."

"We needed a distraction, Jim, nothing more than that. Just another so-and-so to divert attention from the real threat."

"It's not about profit."

"Never."

"And it's not about Mineral X."

"It never was. It's about the thing next to Mineral X. Always has been. It's all that matters. The people, the names, the players, they change every generation. We needed you to distract everybody from the truth."

"The truth," I echoed.

"Now that we've got it, it's the end of the fucking world, Jim. And that's the truth."

"Who are you?"

"All I'll say is, I was born in Stockholm."

Goddamn Polly. Goddamn Diane for being right. It was the Swedes.

"But you're only like nine million people."

"We're very industrious."

"How do I make this stop?"

"You can't. It's inevitable, Jim: death, taxes, and the Swedish ascension." Polly neatly vivisected the meatball on her plate into four quarters with her fork and knife. "Three things you can always count on."

"I don't care about any of that. Kwa Lele's *death*. How do I make *that* stop?"

"You can't stop that either. But I've got an offer for you. You can join her. See her one last time, before you die together."

"Where is she?"

"Dushanbe. Plane ticket is on the table in your CHU. Your flight's at 9 am. Kabul airport's always a bear. You're gonna want to leave extra early to get through security."

36

THE TICKET WAS

The ticket was on the table, as Polly had promised.

I Googled Dushanbe, and it was in Tajikistan, not far from here. I could take the flight, get out of here, I could be free, I could go and rescue Kwa Lele and extradite her to America and then we would escape across the border to live the rest of our lives in Canada.

Sure, she would hate me because I was a man and a white man to boot, just like the one who raped her, but maybe someday she would learn to like me. A little bit. Probably not.

Or I'd die by hanging, I'd be there by her side, she wouldn't die alone, and at least I'd see her one last time.

I could tell her about how I killed Paul, and we'd have a good laugh right before our necks snapped.

Rahim's children would be slaughtered. The insurrection would get put down. They were all doomed to die anyway—the lot of all poor citizens of countries with resources to extract. If it didn't happen now, it would happen later. One decade the Soviets, another decade the Americans, the next decade, Swedes.

Same old story.

I touched the picture Rahim's daughter had made for me, stuck on my CHU refrigerator. It was in one color only: graphite. It was a terrible rendition of the day she'd shown me the heart-shaped leaf. I was a bunch of scribbles, she was a bunch of scribbles. She had no artistic talent whatsoever. The only identifiable part of it was the leaf.

The heart.

"ARE YOU READY?" Rahim asked me. I climbed into that ancient Toyota Corolla one last time.

"No," I said. "Take me to the airport instead."

He searched my face, and I could feel his panic. We were still slightly networked, so he must have known I wasn't serious.

"Just kidding," I said. "Time to die."

"Don't say that," Rahim said. "Nobody is going to die today."

THE DROP SITE—SITE A.

THE INSTRUCTIONS:

1. Park the car by the railing, and
2. wait to receive another text.

Simple enough.

We parked, and we waited. Rahim rattled his loop of beads and mumbled his prayers. I didn't know what I would pray for, if I believed in anything. Just to see Kwa Lele one more time, I suppose. Not even multiple more times.

Because what the hell would I do with her time, besides waste it?

Rahim's phone vibrated on the dash. We both jumped.

BEHIND THE MINE

. . .

"LET'S DO THIS," I said. I was trying to stay cheerful, but we both felt my dread.

I marched into the valley, Rahim behind me, my heart thudding in my chest. Our hands raised to the sky.

Two scrawny men tracked our movements with big, big guns, worn faces, both of them. Kwa Lele would have eaten them for a light afternoon snack if she'd been here. These guys thought I was the enemy and vice versa. We'd all been swindled. My enemy was employed by the same outfit that direct-deposited paychecks into my bank account on a bi-weekly basis, less taxes for social security, health insurance premiums, and other vestiges of civilization.

We got close enough not to run while we stayed far enough to not be a threat.

One man keyed open the trunk of their Toyota Corolla, while the other kept his gun trained on me. Took out a sack. Dumped its contents out on the ground.

Two small bodies.

Rahim broke behind me, a sobbing scream from deep inside.

They didn't rise.

Rahim loosened his clutch on me, made a move towards them.

A staccato blast in the air from the closest gun. I thought I recognized him from the first of our early-stage meetings for inspections training.

Rahim stopped short. The other gunman nudged each tiny mass with his foot and said something I didn't understand.

It was a miracle—Rahim's children stood up. Both of them. The girl fell back down again, bony legs collapsing. I saw her little chest heave.

Rahim and I edged closer.

She had a nosebleed, I saw—her hair was a total rat's nest. How long had they been missing? A day? Two? A lot could happen in two days.

The boy was crying, Rahim was crying. The girl was gasping now, struggling hard to breathe.

Nobody spoke—they said *you come with us* by pointing their guns first at me, then at the children. Two for one.

Even if there was an afterlife, and even if Kwa Lele was hanging by her beautiful neck at the moment of my death and we both wound up in heaven together, my wife and kids would be there too. Super awkward. Nothing ever works out in this world. I couldn't expect things to be any different in the next.

"Let them go," I shouted. "I'll come."

I started down towards them. One step, two steps. I gestured to the children. The men raised their guns, though Rahim and I were still ten yards away, at least. Jumpy. Hired hands, like me and Rahim.

No bosses here, only the help.

"Rahim," I tugged on his arm. "Tell them I'm unarmed. Translate that. Let the kids go, now."

He took his eyes off his children for a moment. I was petrified, now that it came down to it. Now that I had no choice and there was no way out. I passed it off as anger. Spoke louder. "I said, tell them!"

I couldn't get anything done right in this country without Rahim, to the bitter end. He translated for me, his voice breaking. Our captors responded, their eyes on me. They agreed. This was their intended deal, too.

"I'll walk around the other side. Grab your kids and go."

Rahim nodded, his eyes on his children. We split and started walking, slow, hands in the air still, no sudden moves, so they didn't get trigger happy and gun us all down. I walked an arc around to the right.

Kwa Lele, if we live through this, if we somehow get through this mess, or if none of this had ever happened in the first place, in another time and place we still wouldn't wind up together, because I repulse you.

Rahim picked up his daughter, and managed to lift the boy, too. One step, two. I braced for their inevitable gun-down, collapse.

Rahim stumbled faster. Go, go, I willed them. Faster. No shots. Not yet. Then he took off, running, running.

They disappeared over the ridge.

After they were out of sight, my captor thrust the butt of his gun into my stomach.

This was all it took for something in my abdomen to burst,

shadow on the scan

and the fire exploded in my chest

times two, you better get this checked out as soon as you get home, Mr. Schneider

so hard, I couldn't see.

And it was the damndest thing. Before I could see them, I heard them.

James and Allison. Giggling. Right by my side. I turned to—

Shouting.

The men are shouting and it pulls me into the dirt, I'm here. I'm here. I'm face down, the sun on my neck again, I'd blacked out but now I'm awake, I'm on the ground and I can feel it: I'm split open inside. I roll, roll away from the pain but it's *inside* me.

There's nowhere to go and no way to move to remove myself from the pain. I put my head down again, my cheek's in the dirt.

And I see a dust cloud on the horizon.

My insides, a raw rupture. I'm choking up slurry, bubble in my throat. I vomit the bubble up and I slit my eyes open, and I'm staring into my own blood and phlegm and a dark, fatty clump on the ground.

The dust cloud's getting bigger. I spit on the ground and I look up, up some more, stare into that cloud, into its center.

It's horses.

Horses with people on them.

In the center and front of the pack is the biggest white horse.

Cloud of dust, white horse.

Kwa Lele Odoki is there astride it, as crisp and clear as I am dirty and dying.

I can't tell if she sees me. I don't think she does.

She doesn't even squint in the sun. It's like they're made of the same stuff, burning away everything in their path.

Rolling over the horizon, there she is. And a thousand women at her back.

I closed my eyes.

When I opened them again, with great personal effort, the cracked and peeling toes of two old combat boots were inches from my face, all I could see.

"Jim Schneider," Kwa Lele said.

I closed my eyes. I didn't mean to. It was a struggle, everything was a struggle. When I opened them again, the boots were still there. One pointed at me, the other perpendicular.

"If you are so intent upon dying," Kwa Lele said, "Please, go ahead. And if not, you get yourself up. You get yourself up off this ground *right* now. Do you hear me?"

"Yes," I whispered.

"Good," she said. "We have work to do."

THE END

THANKS FOR TAKING

Thanks for taking the time to read my second novel, Love in the Time of the Improvised Explosive Device.

Right now I have one other book available in the New Espionage Series, Corporate Torsos Need Not Apply. The two novels are connected, but you don't have to read them in any particular order.

As ever, if you see any mistakes, plot holes, misspellings, or anything else that would shame a perfectionist, I'd appreciate it if you'd contact me directly via jr@jrpomerantz.com and let me know.

JRP.

QUOTES FROM THE AFGHANISTAN
LISTENING PROJECT

These are some quotes from the Afghanistan Listening Project, conducted in 2009 and published 8 June 2010.

"We did not care much for the vegetables before. An agency taught us about nutrition and how to eat better. Now we try to eat vegetables."
   - Villagers in Badakhshan

"The donor comes to an international NGO, the INGO comes to a local NGO, the local NGO comes to a contractor, the contractor to a sub-contractor and finally we receive nothing."
   - Resident of Kabul

"More money does not represent action."
   - Student at a girl's school, Kabul

"Local NGOs are like robbers. We trust the internationals more, but there is a lot of wastage in international organizations, for example highly paid consultants in the ministries. Some earn $2,000 per day. My boss in the PRT gets $17,000 per month."
   - Afghan journalist in Bamiyan Province

"Donors should come back and see what they have accomplished."
    - Community member in Bamiyan

"It was better under the Russians. At least they checked!"
    - Resident of Kabul

"I was at a meeting with an NGO and I asked 'Is the assistance going to the poorest?' and no one answered."
    - Resident of Kabul

"At the Bonn Conference many countries promised to help because Afghanistan needs assistance. Foreigners come to help poor people. We hear rumors that they are here to take artifacts, but I disagree with them. Still some do have their own purposes."
    - Student at Bamiyan University

"[An INGO] did some bad things here. They smuggled out a lot of artifacts. They were building a road in Chilistoon just so that they could get to a cave and dig the artifacts out. Their Afghan staff saw it...The Taliban are a good excuse for the West to be in Afghanistan. Terrorism is a golden element that allows the Americans to be wherever they want."
    - Afghan journalist in Bamiyan Province

"Poppy politics, poppy policies. Nothing has worked, but why? Where do they export from? I have heard rumors of US air bases. Or maybe the ISI [Pakistan Secret Service]. The security collapse in Afghanistan has happened because we have not targeted the rural population. Seventy percent of the people are landless-farmers. The donors have pushed commercialization of agriculture. Who benefits from that? The landlords. In development plans, good governance is always one pillar. So why does bad governance continue? There's donor pressure, but they don't mean it."
    - Afghan government employee

"There are 150 NGOs in Bamiyan, but we don't know what they do."
   - Faculty member, Bamiyan University

"Agencies brought some projects which are not applicable and not useful in this area, for example, honeybee production. We do not need this, because this area is not appropriate for bees and we can't take care of them. Also, the water storage facility is badly constructed. The water tastes bad after it has been stored."
   - Community members in Badakhshan

"People are happy in their heart, but not impressed with the quality of assistance."
   - Afghan journalist in Bamiyan Province

"Seven years ago, an aid worker asked me what we needed. I told her, 'build a small dam for electricity.' She said no and gave many reasons. We still have no electricity. There was an early failure of the government and internationals to involve the people. That is why we see a gap. The people talked about the economy, while the government and internationals talked about security. They are building services that people cannot afford, like hospitals or schools. If the people cannot afford them, what is the point? Our main product is grapes. We need to invest in water management, cold storage and juice factories."
   - Resident from Mir Bacha Kot, Kabul suburbs

"They dug a well in our village but it doesn't have enough water and we don't have machinery to dig deeper."
   - Villager in Badakhshan

"Where ISAF presence is less, there is more security. They can't supply security for themselves."
   - High school student in Kabul

"Aid closed the mouth of the commanders because they received it."

- Member of Parliament in Kabul

"Too often I see internationals put their foot on people's mouths. They do not listen to us, there is capacity here but it is neglected."
    - Translator working for a bilateral donor in Bamiyan Province

"The experts who come here are not actually professionals."
    - Member of Parliament in Kabul

The whole report is available here.